MYSTERY OF THE EGYPTIAN TEMPLE

Kid Detective Zet

SCOTT PETERS

BDB
FOR YOUNG READERS

Mystery of the Egyptian Temple (Kid Detective Zet Book Three)

Copyright © 2019 Scott Peters and Susan Wyshynski

Library of Congress Control Number: 2019907752

ISBN: 978-0-9859852-5-7 (Hardcover)

ISBN: 978-0-9859852-2-6 (Paperback)

Book cover design by Susan Wyshynski

First printing edition August 2013

Best Day Books For Young Readers

Visit Scott's blog, egyptabout.com, for Ancient Egypt homework resources, free teacher worksheets, mummy facts and more.

ACKNOWLEDGMENTS

So much goes into writing a book, and I could never have done it without the help of the following people. First, I must thank my parents, who have always gone above and beyond to support and encourage me. Thanks to Peter and Judy Wyshynski, to my sisters Jill and Sarah, to Scott Lisetor, Sharon Brown, Amanda Budde-Sung, Ellie Crowe, Adria Estribou, Glenn Desy, and David Desy. And to everyone who had a hand in this novel, and who helped me along the way, I say thank you from the bottom of my heart.

STRANGE VISITORS

Twelve-year-old Zet grabbed at the pair of lean arms that tightened around his neck. He tried to yell, but his yell came out as a gasp. He lurched forward, pulling the boy with him. The two of them fell to the ground. They rolled several times across the sun-scorched paving stones.

With a holler of triumph, Zet yanked himself free.

"I won!" Zet said.

"It's not over yet," shouted his best friend, Hui.

Hui lunged again. The boys were equally matched. Hui usually had some trick up his sleeve but Zet was fast on his toes. He sprinted to the edge of Hui's rooftop. He was two-stories high.

Zet glanced back over his shoulder and then jumped.

He cleared the gap and landed on all fours on the neighbor's roof, just a hand's width from the drop. Behind him, Hui charged and took his own flying leap. Zet headed for the next roof, and then another.

Four rooftops down, he threw a glance backward. Not watching where he was going, he let out an *oof* as he slammed into a tall, soft figure. It was old Teni.

She screeched. The basket of laundry in her arms flew one way, Zet went the other. He landed on his behind and winced.

"What, by the gods, are you doing up here?" she cried. Her cheeks were bright red and her forehead was sweaty under her braided wool wig. She glanced at the top of the neighboring house and spotted Hui, who looked like a guilty dog.

"And you, too!" Teni cried. "Your mothers will hear about this!"

"Sorry," Zet said, and scrambled to his feet. He quickly started gathering Teni's laundry.

"Leave it! Your hands are filthy! Hui, get over here now. Both of you are going back onto the street where you belong."

Shamefaced, Hui came across. Teni ordered them down the hatch. At the bottom of her ladder, she grabbed them by their ears, dragged them through her house, thrust them outside, and slammed her door.

"Oops," Zet said, unable to suppress a grin.

"You can say that again," Hui said. "My mother is going to kill me."

"Well, my mother is baking right now. I say we go to my house and eat cake before she finds out. Because after that, I probably won't be eating cake for weeks."

Hui's eyes lit up. "Cake! Race you!"

Together, they sprinted down the narrow streets of Thebes, laughing. Late afternoon sunlight burned down. Hot, bright rays gave way to cool shadows as they turned into a side street.

It had been weeks since Zet had saved Hui from the whole cursed scarab mystery. The upside was that Zet had his best friend back. Ever since their fathers went to war, life had seemed far too serious. Zet ran the family pottery stall with his younger sister, Kat, while their mother took care of the baby at home. Now, with Hui around, the days the market was closed had become a lot more fun.

The downside was that Hui was out of work. An incredibly skilled novice jeweler, Hui had been the star apprentice at the Kemet workshop. The other downside was that Hui and Zet's sister Kat had huge crushes on each other, which for some weird reason meant that Hui and Kat spent a lot of time arguing—with Zet stuck in the middle.

Go figure.

"Wait till Kat hears about Teni." Hui's grin was a near perfect imitation of his family's household god—Bes—the ancient trickster himself.

"Kat will not want to hear about Teni," Zet said.

"What? Kat will think it's hilarious. She'll love it!"

Zet groaned. He could just picture his younger sister's face. She might only be eleven, but she had a no-nonsense, logical side when it came to anything that might hurt sales at their pottery stall. He could feel a Kat-Hui argument coming on.

"Kat will not love it," he tried to explain. "She thinks upsetting the neighbors is bad for business."

"She'll think it's worth it when I tell her about the look on Teni's face —" Hui paused, staring ahead. "What's going on up there?"

They had just rounded the corner into Zet's street. Two-story, mud brick houses with brightly painted doors lined the well-swept, narrow lane. At the far end, standing in single file before Zet's front steps, stood six uniformed guards.

At first, Zet thought the men were medjay, the city police. But then he saw the heavy weapons on their hips, and the medals that gleamed at their shoulders. Most carried fiber shields, and several wore helmets. Soldiers.

"What are they doing at your place?" Hui said.

Zet walked faster. "I don't know." He broke into a run. Was it possible? Had the thing he wanted most finally come true?

Hui matched him stride for stride. "What do you think they want?"

"Father," Zet gasped, running. "My father must be home! Back from fighting the Hyksos invaders!"

Hui latched onto Zet's arm. He yanked him to a stop. "Wait."

Zet tried to shake him off. "Let go! What are you doing! I haven't seen my father in over a year."

"If your father was home, others would be too. Mine would be, and . . . well . . ."

Zet's expression faltered. A sick feeling grabbed him. He glanced at the soldiers. They stood, arms crossed over their breastplates, and stared stiffly straight ahead.

No, Hui was right. This was no welcome home party. If Father was back, the war would be over, and the whole town would be celebrating.

"That's true." Still, he started forward, a lump in his throat.

"Maybe your father won a medal," Hui said, trying to grin, but his expression was shaky. "And they've come to tell you about it."

Zet nodded, not saying what they both really thought. Medals that arrived like this were bleak things.

"Whatever the reason, I have to know." He approached his door.

Please let father still be alive.

The closest soldier raised a thick arm to bar his way. "Name?"

"Zet, son of Nefer. This is my friend Hui. Why are you here?"

"I am not authorized to say. Please, go inside. They're waiting."

Fearing the worst, Zet stepped through the door. Hui followed and the soldier shut it firmly behind them.

For some reason, the windows had all been fastened tightly shut. After the fierce brightness outside, it took a moment for his eyes to adjust. Not only was the front room unbearably hot, it was crammed with more soldiers.

Kat appeared, maneuvering her way clear of the adults. Zet's sister grabbed his wrist.

"Thank Ra you're here. I was going to come looking for you!" Kat's cheeks were bright. "She's back!"

Zet frowned. "Who's back? Why are the soldiers here?"

"Come on." She dragged him forward.

Zet glanced back at Hui, who looked equally mystified. The soldiers parted to let the three of them through.

Zet spotted his mother first.

"Zet!" she said, sounding relieved.

A cloaked figure sat next to his mother on one of their comfortably worn pillows. The hood fell back when the figure glanced up, revealing a wrinkled, familiar face. The old visitor did not meet his eyes. She couldn't. She was blind.

Hui elbowed Zet hard. "That's the Queen Mother!" he whispered in awe.

"I know," Zet said, grinning.

He breathed a shaky sigh of relief. His father was safe. But why had Pharaoh's mother come?

MISSING

This wasn't the first time the Queen Mother had visited Zet's house. Her appearance amazed him nonetheless.

It was shocking to see a royal figure here, in their front room.

Meanwhile, certainty that this visit had nothing to do with his father caused his heart to stop hammering. The knot in his stomach loosened. He knelt and bowed low.

"Hello, Your Highness," Zet said.

The Queen Mother smiled, focusing her blind gaze where he knelt. "Is that you, my friend?"

"Yes," he said, beaming.

"Please, no kneeling," she said.

How could she tell?

"We know each other too well for that," she said.

Zet rose, but Hui stayed plastered to the floor. The Queen Mother cocked her head to one side as if listening.

"Is someone with you?" she asked.

"My friend, Hui."

"Well, Hui, it's a pleasure to meet you," she said.

Hui jolted as if shocked by the sound of the famous Mother of Egypt's Pharaoh speaking his name. He stuttered out a garbled reply.

"All of you, come sit beside me. I'd like to hear your news. I hear so little of life outside the palace. It's a treat for an old woman like me."

"Come on," Zet whispered, pulling Hui to his feet.

"Sit there?" Hui whispered. "Beside the Queen Mother?"

"She won't bite," Kat whispered, at Hui's elbow.

"I might, unless you hurry," the Queen Mother said. She had sharp ears.

Hui winced. "Sorry, Your Highness."

It was easy for Zet and Kat to act nonchalant. They'd helped her in the past, and she'd rewarded them with a huge chest of gold deben. Still, Zet's nonchalant attitude was partly an act. He remained in as much awe as Hui, but it was fun watching Hui's reaction.

The Queen Mother reached forward blindly, found a cushion and patted it. "Here. Come. Tell me how you've been. And then I'll explain why I'm here."

At first, Zet couldn't help feeling formal. But soon, they were talking and laughing about things that had happened since they'd last seen one another. Zet told her about the pottery he had purchased with her reward to restock his family stall.

The Queen Mother told him that everyone in the palace was now regularly eating the chickpea salad recipe she'd gotten from Zet's mother.

"It is wonderful to come here, away from the palace and its busy intrigues," the Queen Mother said. "You are blessed in this home."

Zet nodded. He knew the time had come for the truth of her visit. "Highness, why are you here? What's happened?"

In her lap, her bony fingers tightened around an object fastened to a golden chain. The color drained from her frail cheeks. She looked afraid and suddenly fragile. Something was wrong. Very wrong.

"Zet, I'd like to speak to you alone," she said.

Kat and Hui scrambled to their feet. Meanwhile, she raised her blind eyes to the soldiers in the room. "My good men, please, give us some space."

"But My Lady!" said the closest soldier, one hand on his gilded sword hilt. "Do you know where we are?"

"Yes," she said drily. "I know exactly where we are. As I recall, I provided the directions."

Zet and Hui grinned at each other.

"Of course you did, what I mean is—well, Madam, the neighborhood, it's not safe for you!"

"I trust you will protect me should any harm arise," she said with an amused smile.

"She's been in worse places," Zet couldn't help adding.

At this, the Queen Mother laughed out loud. "Indeed I have."

After the soldiers left, and Kat and Hui had retreated to the kitchen, she turned to Zet.

"What I'm about to share, you must not tell anyone," she said.

"I understand."

Worry lines creased her face. "You're familiar with my oldest granddaughter?"

He nodded. "Princess Meritamon."

"And you know her birthday is coming up?"

"Yes," Zet said, wondering where this was leading. "Definitely. I hear it's going to be amazing. The whole city is looking forward to the celebration."

"There may not be one," the Queen Mother said.

"What? Why not?"

"Princess Meritamon is missing."

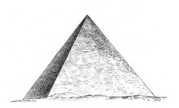

A ROYAL SPY

Zet stared at the Queen Mother in shock.

Missing? He'd never met the Princess, despite his friendship with Pharaoh's famous mother. Like the rest of Thebes, he'd only glimpsed her from a distance. His mind flew back to the last time he'd seen her—at the Opet Festival, just over three weeks ago. There had been a chariot race, with crowds lining the Boulevard of the Sphinx.

Princess Meritamon sat in the large royal booth; like Hui had pointed out, it was hard *not* to notice her. She was thirteen, going on fourteen. One year older than Zet. She'd been seated next to her half-sister, Sitamun.

The half-sisters were the same age, but nothing alike.

Sitamun was pale and quiet, like her nickname—daughter of the moon.

When Zet thought of Meritamon, he pictured a girl who practically sparkled when she laughed. She had this bubbling energy that drew your attention. When a chariot rider nearly crashed during a daring play to pass his opponent, instead of shrinking back, she'd actually shouted with delight.

Kat said Princess Meritamon was the prettiest girl in Egypt. The Princess seemed almost unconscious of the fact. Mostly she seemed interested in people. She'd tilt her head to listen when someone spoke to her, and her eyes would light up when she was talking. Zet couldn't help wondering what it would be like to meet face to face.

Apparently, he wasn't alone. Pharaoh's guests had seemed more interested in having the Princess include them in her circle than watching the chariot race. As did the people in the streets. They'd shout her name, which would make her laugh in apparent surprise, and then she'd wave.

Zet came back to the present, his mind spinning.

Missing?

But she must have been guarded; the royal family was under constant protection!

"How can she be missing?" he asked.

"It's the same question I've been asking myself. And it's the reason I'm here." The Queen Mother squared her shoulders to face him. "I need you to help me find out what happened. I need you to help bring my granddaughter home."

Zet stared at her in disbelief. "Me?"

"Oh, we have medjay police working on the case, but you have something unique. You can get into places others can't. Many adults don't believe children know much." She smiled, looking rueful. "They're willing to let their guard down, and say things they wouldn't dare tell a man in uniform."

"That's true," Zet said with a laugh. "You wouldn't believe some of the things people discuss in front of us at the stall. Like we're not even there."

"They were children once. You'd think they'd remember how it was."

Footsteps moved across the upper floor. His mother was busy doing some chores.

Zet shifted on his cushion, wanting to ask something but worried about offending her. "This might sound crazy, but—"

"Tell me."

"Well, is it possible she went off on her own? For a day or two?"

"Meritamon is certainly capable of such mischief. She enjoys raising a little trouble now and then—not that I didn't at her age! But no. First, she wasn't in Thebes. And second, we have proof she was kidnapped."

"Kidnapped." Shock ran through him. "Where was she?"

"At Abydos. Pharaoh's building a new temple there. Merit went seven days ago by boat for a small vacation," the Queen Mother said, using the princess's shortened name. "She was to tour the project, and then meet with her father as he came south from the battlefront." Her voice became quiet. "They planned to travel back here together for her birthday celebration."

Zet swallowed. The darkness and heat of the room felt suffocating. "If Princess Merit was kidnapped, is there a ransom?"

"A terrible one. But there's no time to go into it now. You'll hear it soon enough."

Zet frowned, wondering what she meant by that.

"Only a few people know, that's why I sent my soldiers out of the room. Merit went to Abydos disguised as a priestess. She is Pharaoh's heir. We are at war. If word spreads of her disappearance, fear would spread with it. It would be seen as a terrible omen."

"Can't you just pay the ransom?" he said, wondering why the Queen Mother would do anything besides that.

"Gladly! If it were gold. The kidnappers don't want gold. They want our army to give up the battle and let the invading forces take over our country. My granddaughter has been kidnapped by the Hyksos. She's become a piece in a game of war."

It was the worst blow Zet could ever imagine. "What is Pharaoh doing? He must be tearing Abydos apart."

"No, he can't."

Zet stared at her in shock.

"We've been warned by the kidnappers that if Pharaoh launches a full scale military search, my granddaughter will be killed immediately. That's why I sent only a small contingent of medjay." Her voice faltered. All her steely reserve threatened to break, and a glimpse of complete and utter despair showed through. She was simply a grandmother whose granddaughter has been snatched away. "We must find her. We can't let them win. Not now."

"She'll be found," Zet said, even though he had no idea if it were true.

The Queen Mother reached for his hand and squeezed it. Her fingers looked frail, but there was strength in them.

"I'll do anything," Zet said. "Tell me what you want me to do."

"I want you to go to Abydos."

Abydos. Zet's heart leapt at the thought. It was a far off place he'd only heard about in stories. A place Pharaoh Ahmose had chosen as his eternal burial site. Remote and far from any village or town, it would be unlike anything he could imagine.

Of course he wanted to go. It was his duty. But what about the pottery stall? Taking care of his family was his duty, too. His mother and Kat needed him here. He couldn't just leave.

"I know you run a good business, and I'm asking a lot of you. I've already talked to your mother," the Queen Mother said. "I offered to have my own people help out at your stall. She told me she would work things out."

"Then, yes. Of course. I'll do it."

"Just be my eyes and ears up there. I've assigned you to work for the head architect as a runner. Keep watch, and report what you see to him. Anything you learn will be passed on to the men leading the investigation."

"I can do that."

"Good. Remember, watch and listen, nothing more. I have no intention of putting you at risk. Any questions?"

"I have a request."

"Name it."

"I want Hui to go with me."

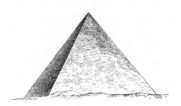

4

ROYAL TOKENS

Zet watched the Queen Mother's face. Would she let Hui go with him? Would she trust a second person, someone she didn't know? He pictured traveling all that way without a friend to run ideas with, with no one at his back. He didn't like it. With Hui, he stood a chance of succeeding. Without him, he wasn't so sure.

Finally, she said, "This is a dangerous mission, I have no right to ask even you to go."

"I want to." And he did. Either way, he'd go.

"All right." Her face looked fierce and full of hope. "I think bringing Hui is a good idea. You'll have someone to rely on. If he's able, I'm in favor. It's safer than you being alone. But we need to act quickly. The boat's waiting."

Zet stood. "I'll tell him."

At that moment, Zet's mother came down the steps from their sleeping quarters—which for Kat and Zet was usually the roof. They liked to sleep up there on hot nights, under the winking stars.

She held a sack. "I hope I've put enough things in here."

"I promise, whatever's missing can be provided at Abydos," the Queen Mother said. "But I must trouble you with another request."

After the Queen Mother explained, Zet's mother nodded.

"I think I can convince Hui's mother, Delilah, without giving too much away. Even still, she's no gossip. She'd never tell a soul. And she'll probably be glad to see Hui busy."

"It's a lot to ask, to put your son and hers in danger," the Queen Mother said.

"These are dangerous times," she said softly.

Zet flashed on his future. He'd rarely slept away from home. And never without his family. The few times he'd traveled had been to buy pottery at the potter's village downriver. Despite the seriousness of his task, and his fear for the Princess, he felt suddenly alive. More alive than he'd ever felt.

Bastet's whiskers!

This was going to be an adventure.

MOMENTS LATER, a confused looking Hui was called out of the kitchen where he'd been waiting with Kat. He stammered out his goodbyes to the Queen Mother, still clueless as to what was going on. How Zet hoped he could come!

"Meet you at the harbor," Zet's mother said, leaving with Kat, Hui and Zet's baby brother.

The Queen Mother turned to Zet. "I have some things for you." She rummaged in a soft, calfskin satchel stamped with the royal insignia and pulled out a leather tube. "These are your work papers. Show them to Senna, the architect, when you arrive."

He took the small, leather tube and pulled off its cap.

A scroll lay nestled inside. He tipped it out into his palm. A wax blob sealed the smooth, finely burnished papyrus. Stamped into the blob was a fancy cartouche. He moved his fingers over the raised hieroglyphics, awed to be holding such a thing.

"That's my personal seal. It reads, Tetisheri—my birth name. Don't let anyone see it, except the architect. Otherwise, your cover will be blown and the game will be up."

"I won't."

"The other thing I want to give you is this." She opened her frail right hand and Zet saw what she'd been holding all this time. The golden chain held a ring. She found Zet's hand and pressed it into his palm. "Guard it carefully."

The ring felt warm. Made of thick gold, it looked ancient. "Wait. Is this . . .?"

"My coronation ring."

"But Your Highness—" His head spun with the enormity of this thing in his fingers. "With respect, don't ask me to take this."

"You're going as my spy. Only one person at Abydos knows this, and that's Senna the architect. Should anything happen to him, you'll be on your own. In a situation like this, things could turn bad quickly. If you need to demand passage home—or if your actions raise too many questions with the medjay, this is your safeguard. Use it only if you need to! And hide it wisely."

He didn't move. "Highness, I can't take it."

"I won't send you without it. Put the chain around your neck."

Stiffly, he did as he was told. It felt heavy against his chest. Filled with a worry he couldn't define, he tucked the royal coronation symbol into the front of his tunic. The ring felt like it held the power of the gods. And in a way it did, for the Queen Mother was a living god on earth.

She touched his head. "May the hidden powers of Egypt keep you safe."

IN THE STREET, Zet set off at a run.

An hour ago, he'd been worried about old Teni getting him in trouble for charging across her rooftop. Now, he was being sent on a quest to find a missing princess. Fresh excitement surged through him.

It struck him suddenly that he'd forgotten all about the honey cakes his mother had been baking. His stomach roared. He hadn't eaten since breakfast, and they were his favorite. No doubt Hui had eaten half a dozen while he was in the kitchen with Kat.

Too bad he hadn't stuffed one in his bag!

Zet reached the dock out of breath.

Numerous ships bobbed nearby. Kat, his mother and baby Apu stood at the appointed location. And with them, stood Hui.

Zet whooped and pumped his arm in the air. "Yes!"

"Adventure twins!" Hui said, and raised both hands.

They fist bumped each other.

Zet glanced at Kat, who looked considerably less excited. In fact, she looked downright glum.

"What's wrong?" Zet asked her. "Is it because you're not coming?"

Hui winced. "Kat, I didn't mean—"

Kat crossed her arms and her cheeks turned bright red. She made a point of ignoring him, and said to Zet, "I could care less about coming. Not when you're going to save *'the most beautiful girl in the world'*, like Hui said."

Hui had his hands clutched in his hair. "The most beautiful *princess* in the world," he said in a whisper.

Kat glared.

Zet choked back a laugh. Hui was just digging himself deeper.

Looking frantic, Hui said, "She's probably all looks. She's probably nowhere near as smart as you, Kat."

"That's what you have to say? That I'm smart?"

Zet groaned. Usually Kat liked being called smart. But clearly right now that was not the case. Girls were weird. Then again, so were boys, according to the ridiculous expression on Hui's face. Zet's best friend looked confused and desperate.

Trying to save him, Zet said, "Is that our boat?"

ALL ABOARD

Birds screeched and dove over the Nile's broad expanse. A breeze whipped across the shimmering surface, ruffling the moving currents. Nearby, fishermen offloaded nets of silver perch. The air smelled of seafood and wood-sealing pitch.

Zet and the others stood on the wharf, surveying the lineup of boats. Zet's mother ignored the argument between Kat and Hui. Instead, she was reading a set of instructions.

"I believe it's the furthest one down. Come on."

Clearly glad for the change of subject, Hui said. "Wow, we're going on that boat?"

"It's huge," Zet said. "Has to be longer than eight cows standing nose to tail!"

"Acacia wood construction. See that, Kat?" Hui said, looking hopefully at her. "They make wood bricks and glue them together with reeds and sap."

Kat looked at the boat but said nothing.

On board, men moved everywhere on deck. Some tied down crates. Others fitted jutting oars into place. Still others tightened down the square sail that flew from the center mast. Tattoos covered their thick arms, and their sun-darkened faces were like leather. It was clear everyone spent day and night outside. The only structure was a small cabin mid-ship, which was surely reserved for the Captain.

Already Zet's heart was leaping with the thrill of adventure.

The last two times he'd been involved in a mystery, Kat had helped. She must be feeling left out. He would be.

"Kat." He grabbed her elbow. "Thanks for managing the stall. It might be the boring part of this job, but it's just as important. I couldn't go without you here."

Kat let out the breath she'd been holding, and beamed for real. "Thanks."

Hui approached Kat. "You won't forget me, will you?"

Zet couldn't help snorting. "We're only going for a few days, we're not coming back as graybeards."

Meanwhile, Kat seemed to have softened somewhat. Zet thought she might be preparing to throw her arms around Hui's neck in a farewell hug.

"Please tell me you're not still mad," Hui said.

Kat twined her fingers together.

"She might be beautiful," Hui said in sudden earnest. "But your braids are longer. Much longer!"

At this, Kat's forehead scrunched up and her mouth opened. The color started to rise in her cheeks again and she dropped her arms to her sides. She never managed to get out what she was about to say, because Zet cut in.

"We have to go!"

"Zet's right," their mother agreed.

Hui, however, was busy leaping about and making funny faces at Kat, trying to make her laugh. She wouldn't have any of it.

From the ship's rail above, a deep voice boomed, "What's going on? You boys boarding today or not?"

Zet looked up to see a man who had to be the Captain. His eyes were hard, like two black onyx stones. The man gripped the rail with meaty fingers and glared down at them.

"Yes!" Zet called. "We're coming up. Right now."

"Maybe you should leave your buddy behind. He looks thick in the head."

Hui stopped capering and put his fists on his hips. "I am not thick in the head."

"Are too," Kat said.

Zet's mother said, "My apologies, Captain. We didn't mean to keep you waiting." She herded the boys toward the gangplank. "Now, watch your manners and everything will be fine. And don't forget to bundle up at night. It can be cold this time of year. I've packed several tunics, along with a pair of your father's old sandals in case—"

"Don't worry, Mother. We'll manage," Zet said, hugging her and grinning.

A moment later, he and Hui hopped off the gangplank onto the warm deck.

Deeply tanned sailors started pulling in ropes.

Zet glanced around and saw that he and Hui weren't the only guests on board. A small crowd of passengers was also headed for Abydos. To one side stood an ominous looking priest. His shaved head glistened with oil and dark energy seemed to swirl around him; probably because he was murmuring strange words and staring with glazed eyes at the horizon.

Nearby—but keeping their distance from the daunting holy man—sat a dozen or so construction workers. Zet knew they were construction workers by their toolboxes, which most men were using as seats. On one box, a big man sat sharpening a bronze chisel. He looked hot and impatient.

The Captain's wide torso cut off the view. Zet looked up into the man's creased face.

"State your names," the Captain growled.

They did.

"Well, Zet and Hui. We're late. I had to hold my boat." One thumb tucked into his waistband, he eyed them with distaste. "I'd like to know why."

Zet hadn't expected this. Was the man suspicious about holding the ship for two kids, or just annoyed? The Queen Mother's ring on its chain felt suddenly heavy and huge against Zet's chest, as though it were visible through his tunic.

"We're replacing someone," Zet said quickly.

"We just found out," Hui added. "We came right away."

The Captain's dark eyes swept over them as if he knew something wasn't quite right. His lip curled in a snort. Abruptly, he turned and shouted, "Prepare to cast off." To the boys, he said, "Move to the aft deck."

"Will do," Zet said, glad to be relieved of the Captain's scrutiny.

As soon as the Captain left, Hui whispered. "Uh, which way is the aft deck?"

"No idea. Let's just get out of here."

6

NO TURNING BACK

Zet and Hui clambered over ropes, past the central cabin, and headed as far from the gruff Captain as they could get. Only when they reached the curving prow did Zet stop. A trickle of sweat ran down his ribs. He held his pack closer, thinking of the scroll inside, and then of the valuable coronation ring around his neck. He felt like a walking booby trap. Any moment, someone could find either.

In a low voice, Zet said, "We need to put up a good front if we're going to stay undercover."

But Hui wasn't listening. He was belly up to the rail, giving Kat the most pathetic look ever. "She's never going to speak to me again."

"Good," Zet said. "Then I won't have to listen to you fight anymore." He waved at his family. "Anyway, we have more important things to think about right now."

Sailors let out the sail. Wind caught the giant square of linen with a snap. It bowed outward, and the boat jumped away from shore. Zet grabbed the boat's side for support. The wake sent dark ripples weaving across the river's smooth surface.

To Hui, he said, "We need to keep our wits about us. Starting right now."

Hui finally focused on him. "Of course we're keeping our wits."

"What I mean is, we have to act like we're going to Abydos to work. We need to get our story straight. So when people ask what we're doing, we have something to say."

"Right. Of course—putting on my Secret Agent Assistant Hat now," Hui said.

"Don't even say that word."

"What, secret agent?"

"I'm serious!" Zet whispered. "Quit it or I'm dumping you in the Nile right now while you can still swim to shore."

"Oh, great friend you are. Ditch me at the first sign of trouble." But Hui was laughing. "Fine. I like it, having a story. Always good to have a story. So what's ours?"

"We're going as runners for the Head Architect."

"How did we get the job?" Hui asked.

"Through my father. They're old friends, and the architect wants to help my family by giving me work. You're coming because he needed two boys, and I suggested you."

"Wait, your father knows the architect?"

Zet gave Hui a playful punch and laughed. "No!"

"Oh! Right, of course not," Hui said. "Pretty convincing, you were right then. I believed you." He leapt up. "Now that's settled, I'm going to have a look around this ship."

Zet wrapped a protective arm over his satchel and nodded. "I'll catch up with you. I need to sort something out first."

Before turning to go, Hui shot one last longing glance at the shore. Zet followed his best friend's gaze. From this distance, Kat, Zet's mother and baby Apu looked like three tiny grains of wheat. Like the wind could blow them away into nothing.

Zet felt his stomach tighten. He realized it was the first time he'd left them home alone. What if something happened? What if something happened to the pottery stall? He'd sworn to his father he'd protect them, and here he was leaving to solve someone else's problem. Yet it was Pharaoh's problem—the Great Bull, the living god himself. What choice did he have?

Zet wiped the sweat from his palms on his kilt. His family would be fine. He'd see them in a week. What could possibly happen to them in Thebes?

From amid ship, a rowdy bark of laughter issued from the seated workers.

"Well, see you over there," Hui said. Still looking glum about Kat, he tore himself from the rail and headed for the men.

Zet untied his satchel and dug through it until he saw the scroll nestled in the bottom. It seemed unlikely anyone on board would search his bag. They'd never suspect he had anything worth stealing. Still, to have it just lying in there seemed incredibly risky. Better to hide it someplace. Worst case, if it was found, no one could tie the Queen Mother's letter to him, and he'd still have a chance of doing his job.

But if the scroll were found in his personal possession, it would all be over.

His thoughts shifted to the sailors. If this boat went back and forth often—ferrying workmen to the building site—could any of the sailors be involved in the kidnapping? If they were and they found the scroll, not only would the ruse be over, something worse could happen. He and Hui might end up as crocodile food.

Zet glanced around the deck.

The smell of oiled wood and the creak of the sail filled his senses. This boat was a foreign world. Ropes that lay coiled now probably wouldn't stay that way for long, so they wouldn't make a good hiding place.

Would any place be safe?

Butted up against the cabin lay a rowboat made of reeds all lashed together. The boat was upside down. Zet peered under it, and decided it wouldn't do. What if someone used it partway through the journey to ferry someone to shore? Or go fishing?

He moved on, and stopped next to a large wooden crate. Lifting the lid, the earthy smell of onions rose to greet him. The box was heavily loaded. They'd only be on the boat until tomorrow. They'd never eat all these.

A glance told him the coast was clear. The center cabin blocked his view of the men. Still, he'd have to act fast. Heart pounding, he dug deep and fast, shoving onions aside until he could see the crate's bottom. Zet thrust the scroll inside.

His fingers went to the front of his tunic where the Queen Mother's ring lay concealed. The chain felt like a noose around his neck. He began to remove it, but something stopped him. He couldn't shove something so holy in this crate.

Reluctantly, he let go, and then piled the vegetables over the scroll. Soon the leather tube disappeared from view, buried deep. Zet dropped the lid.

The sense of being watched made him jolt upright.

He peered both ways, but saw no one. Heart slamming, he stood. Not a soul in sight. He backed up and wiped sweat from his brow.

The boat rocked under his feet as he set off to find Hui.

The oars had been pulled in, and the oarsmen seats were empty. A steady breeze had caught the square sail, pulling it tight. The powerful ship leaned into the wind and picked up speed. Wood groaned and water churned alongside. The shores reeled past as the boat began its journey northward.

On the left riverbank he could see lush farms close to shore, bordered by desert and a backdrop of steep, rocky mountains. On the right bank, the city gleamed with sparkling monuments and crawled with people going about their business.

It felt refreshing to be detached from it all, flying north in a swift, modern ship.

Zet decided to forget the scroll and his worries and enjoy himself.

There was nothing he could do about the Princess's disappearance right now. Who knew when he'd get to relax again? Tomorrow they'd be landing at Abydos, and then the chase would be on.

A FAMILIAR FACE

Zet edged along deck past the cabin, holding the rail to keep steady. The ship's sway would take getting used to. He headed for the knot of construction workers. They were laughing— deep throated rumbles and guffaws.

Hui stood between the men, dwarfed by their size.

Hui turned and the workers did the same. Zet was pinpointed with a dozen stares. The men were all huge and scarred from work—and maybe fighting, too. Puckered burn marks ran down one man's muscled fore-arms. Another had poorly healed gashes. All had calloused hands with bruised, blackened fingernails. At least half looked to be the kind that turned from laughter to brawling at the first sign of offense.

"Zet, look who's here, can you believe it?"

Zet glanced at the man, but didn't recognize him.

"It's Jafar!" Hui said, "From the Kemet workshop. Jafar, this is my best friend, Zet."

The Kemet Workshop? Instantly, Zet went on alert. Thoughts of the events that had nearly killed Hui flashed through his mind.

"Nice to meet you," Zet said, feeling wary.

"Same." Jafar stuck out a thick hand and they shook. He was missing his little finger. His right eyelid drooped, which made him look like he was winking. But he wasn't, and probably never had. "A pal of Hui's is a pal of mine."

The circle closed around Zet.

"So . . ." Jafar said in a way that suggested he was sizing Zet up. "I hear you two are on a big job."

Inwardly, Zet winced. What was Hui telling them? He tried to keep his face neutral as he shot Hui a look.

"You know, working for the head architect," Hui said. "We're going to be pretty important."

"You couldn't make me give up my craft to be a runner," Jafar said with a snort.

Hui colored. "No," he said quietly. "Well, you take what you can get. Beggars can't be choosy."

Jafar nodded. "Now that's the truth, isn't it? I've been out of work since that whole cursed amulet business."

"Jafar was one of Kemet's master jewelers," Hui told Zet.

"You, my friend, weren't so bad yourself," Jafar said. "Yep. Kemet was worried some jealous apprentice would slit your throat in your sleep and kill his upcoming star! Turns out it was all pointless. We all ended up on the street, didn't we?" He cracked his knuckles and grinned. "But things are looking up."

Zet frowned at the master jeweler. "I don't understand, you'll be making jewelry at the temple?"

The men all barked with laughter.

"No. Hinges and door handles, decorative ornamentation and the like," Jafar said.

"Oh. Right," Zet said, and laughed.

Jafar scratched his chin, then tapped Zet's chest with a thick finger. "You aren't that kid who helped the medjay, are you?"

Another man spoke up. "You sayin' this boy here works with the medjay?"

To Zet's horror, Hui gave a broad grin of acknowledgment, looking ridiculously proud and important. "My buddy Zet here, he's—"

"Way too dumb for something like that," Zet said with a weak laugh. "Me, work with the medjay? That's crazy. Right Hui?"

"Er, right."

Zet managed to pull Hui aside.

"By the gods, Hui, you almost gave us away!" he said.

Hui frowned. "What are you talking about? Don't worry. These men are friends."

"The only friends on this boat are you and me. Everyone else is either a suspect, or a potential danger."

"How? They weren't at the temple. How could they be suspects?"

"All right. Maybe not, but the sailors could be. And the Captain. They've been up and down the Nile ferrying workers."

"That grumpy old Captain, I wouldn't put it past him," Hui said. "Have you seen his smile? I think he's part crocodile."

At this, Zet broke out laughing. "Yes! I think you're right!"

Hui pointed toward shore. "Look at that!" Thebes was fading into the distance and an enormous stone structure had come into view. "The Karnak Temple complex."

The boys leaned on the rail, elbow to elbow, and watched it drift past. At their backs, the sun hung low in the sky. The sun god's slanting rays colored the Karnak temples and monuments with a wash of deep red.

The colossal structures gave way to tilled farmland. Hui settled down and opened his bag. He laid out various pieces of wood, including a bunch of small pegs and two long slats. On one slat, three mischievous faces had been carved in a row. With deft strokes of his knife, Hui began forming a fourth face. It was amazing to watch it appear out of nothing.

"My little brothers," Hui said, grinning as he worked.

"What are you making?"

"It's a lock," Hui said.

"A lock?" Zet had heard of locks, but had never actually seen one.

"It's for mother, for our front door. Look, I'll show you how it works."

The strange priest seated nearby inched closer. "Where did you learn this art?"

"At a jeweler's workshop," Hui said. Kneeling forward, he laid two long slats of wood on deck. Crosswise, he placed several small, duck-bone sized pegs. "These pegs will be the teeth inside, also known as tumblers, which will be inserted right here. To open the lock, a person will need a wooden rod, specially shaped to fit inside and lift the tumblers. It's very secure."

Despite his narrow, haughty face, the priest looked impressed.

Zet was. "Maybe you can make one for my stall, and I can lock up some of our pottery at night. Instead of just covering it with linen like we do now."

Hui nodded. "Done." His face colored. "If I do that, do you think Kat will forgive me?"

8

PLAYING WITH FIRE

It was dusk when the Captain guided the boat toward shore. Rushes slid against the wooden hull. Sailors jumped out, splashing through the marshy shallows and then hauling on ropes until the boat came to rest against the soft sand. Stars had begun to wink overhead, and cool air settled on Zet's shoulders.

"Out 'o my way," a man grumbled at Zet, who'd been leaning protectively against the vegetable crate where he'd hidden the scroll.

Zet jumped aside, panic stricken when the man raised the lid. The man took out an armful of onions, let the lid slam down and made for land. Breathing a sigh of relief, he and Hui went onshore to find dinner. Zet, for one, was starving.

They pounded down the gangplank toward the fire flickering on the beach.

It was pitch dark by the time food was handed out. Bowls of hot stew and bread. Silence fell as everyone set to eating.

"It's really good," Zet said, after his first few pangs of hunger had been sated.

The cook looked up from his dinner and shot him a toothy grin.

"That it is," said the Captain, raising a thick slice of bread in a toast. "Here's to the cook who keeps my men from jumping ship."

"Hear, hear!" shouted the sailors with a roar of laughter.

In a low voice, Jafar said to Hui, "Ah, but the bread's not as good as our old baker friends', now is it?"

Zet caught a strange expression on Jafar's face. Again, he got that unsettling feeling about Hui's old workmate.

Hui sounded uncomfortable as he said, "Those bakers sure had a way with dough."

Jafar guffawed.

On the circle's far side, the Captain stoked the fire with a long branch. Sparks flew, crackling high into the night sky. The red, dancing flames threw shadows and light wavering over the scarred, dark faces of the men. Zet wondered what Kat would think of such a sight. She'd probably cower in terror. He grinned.

Feeling suddenly brave, he got to his feet.

Now was as good a time as any to question the Captain. Maybe the man knew something about Princess Merit's disappearance.

"Going somewhere?" Jafar asked.

Zet shrugged. "Just want to thank the Captain for his hospitality."

Jafar raised one brow.

Trying to look nonchalant, Zet made his way round the fire pit. The closer he got to the Captain, the weaker his legs felt. *Get it together,* he told himself. The Queen Mother hired him for a reason. It was time to start working.

The Captain stiffened as Zet approached. Between his bushy brows, the V-shaped crease deepened and the corners of his mouth turned down.

"I don't brook complaints after hours," he growled.

"I didn't come to complain, I wanted to say sorry for making you wait earlier. Thanks again." He nodded at the big vessel. "That's a really nice boat."

He grunted. "Best on the river."

"How does it compare to the royal barges?" Zet said.

"What kind of question is that?"

Zet raised his hands. "Just asking. I don't know much about boats."

The Captain's shoulders relaxed a little. "I've never been on a royal barge. But mine's the latest in shipbuilding."

It struck Zet that it must have cost a small fortune to build. Did he really make that much as a ferryman? "I guess you ferry a lot of people."

He nodded. "I do."

"Mostly to Abydos, then?"

"Right now, yes."

"How's it going up there?" Zet tried to lead the conversation around to the Princess. "Any trouble we should know about?"

The Captain's eyes narrowed. "What are you getting at?"

Zet shrugged. "They just hired us last minute. It seemed strange. I'm wondering what kind of work I'm headed for, that's all."

The Captain nodded, slowly. "I see. Want a piece of advice?"

Zet opened his mouth to answer, but paused at the look on the Captain's face.

"Stop asking questions," the Captain said.

"But I just—"

The Captain got to his feet, gripping his mug of beer in his meaty fist. "Kontar!"

The nearest sailor cracked his knuckles. "Problem, Captain?"

"There will be, Kontar, unless you take care of this kid."

"Gladly." Kontar grabbed Zet roughly by the neck and towed him away. "My Captain don't like you."

"I was only—"

"Shut it, kid."

Kontar's fingers tightened around Zet's throat. He shoved him along in front of him. The further they got from the fire, the more Zet started to panic.

"Let go," Zet managed, choking and trying to wrench free.

The man's circling grip narrowed like a rope being pulled tight. Zet couldn't believe it—this was crazy. Was the sailor strangling him?

"Stop!"

"I ain't done with you, yet."

Blackness crept around the edge of Zet's vision. He clawed at Kontar's fingers and arms. This was no joke. If Kontar didn't let go soon—

"Let 'im go," came Jafar's voice.

Kontar spun, keeping his hold on Zet. Jafar strode toward them with Hui sprinting alongside. Kontar's grip didn't loosen. Zet was losing consciousness.

"I said let 'im go," Jafar growled.

Kontar laughed. "Says who?"

"Says me and my brothers," Jafar snarled. "We stick together."

As if to prove it, two more construction workers moseyed toward them.

Kontar snorted. "I wasn't hurting the little brat. Just giving him a fright."

He boxed Zet's ear hard. Then Zet was stumbling free. His hands flew to his windpipe. He gasped, sucking in deep breaths. A fright? If Jafar hadn't shown up, Kontar could have killed him! For what? Asking questions?

Kontar hooked one thumb into his knife-belt. "Have a nice night," he sneered, nodding at Zet.

Zet knew then that the danger wasn't over—just postponed. He kept his face blank, hiding his fear, but knew he'd made a dangerous enemy. Why? What were they up to?

When Kontar left, Jafar fastened his drooping eye on Zet. "What's going on?"

"Nothing," Zet said, too quickly.

"Brothers don't keep secrets," Jafar said in a menacing voice.

"No secrets here," Zet lied, rubbing his throat.

"Look at his face," Hui said, grinning. "You think he has a secret worth keeping? Zet? Most boring kid around. He'd be nowhere without me."

"Er . . . Right," Zet said, deciding Hui was laying it on a bit thick.

Jafar laughed, but his droopy eye wasn't smiling. Studying Zet's face, he grunted.

As they made their way on ship, Zet felt the weight of the mystery looming over him, dark and horribly complicated. He needed to know more about Kontar and the Captain. But how?

He felt like an idiot for accepting the Queen Mother's request. He'd been all puffed up with pride. Sure he'd solved a crime or two before, but he'd been lucky. It was easy to solve crimes back home where he knew people, knew the streets, and knew the medjay. Here, he knew no one.

Except Hui, of course.

A glance at his best friend lifted Zet's spirits. He wasn't alone. Thank the gods he had Hui along. Still, they couldn't talk with Jafar between them.

Until they could talk, he'd just have to puzzle things out on his own. Questions ran through his mind. What had made the Captain and Kontar so angry? What were they hiding? He ran a hand over his throat. There was something shifty going on.

And what about this expensive boat?

How had the Captain paid for it? With Hyksos bribes?

Still, if the Captain was the kidnapper, where would he be hiding the Princess?

9

NORTHWARD

et, Hui and Jafar had only been on board several moments when raucous voices filled the air. Both craftsmen and sailors were returning. Their footsteps shook the gangway and the boat rocked under their weight.

Hui sat in the prow. "Do you think Kat's still mad at me?"

"Are we back on that subject?" Zet smothered a grin. Hui looked miserable and Zet's heart went out to him.

"It's not funny," Hui said in a glum voice. "Just wait until you like a girl. Then we'll see who's laughing."

"Ha! After watching you two, I probably never will."

Jafar belched and rubbed his belly. "Girls are trouble."

The rest of the construction crew joined them on the forward deck. Zet suddenly felt glad of their presence. At least with them nearby, Kontar would have a hard time getting Zet and Hui alone.

"I'm beat," Jafar announced. He made for the overturned rowboat, raised it with his four-fingered right hand and peered underneath. "Looks like I found a bedroom."

Zet said a silent prayer of thanks that he hadn't hidden the scroll there.

Meanwhile, the other workmen staked out spots against the

bulwarks and the Captain's cabin wall. The air had grown chill. Blankets were tugged out of packs. Zet found the neatly folded cover his mother had provided. It smelled of home—of his mother's soap. He held it tight around him and lay down with his back to the crate that hid the scroll. Despite his worries, he soon slipped off into a deep, dreamless sleep.

THE SOUND of gently lapping water woke him.

Grey dawn stretched overhead. He stared up at the sky. This wasn't his rooftop. He frowned, momentarily confused. His neck hurt.

Then it all came rushing back. The Queen Mother's visit, the boat, the run-in with the Captain and Kontar. He sat up and touched his throat. It felt sore and tender. Around him the construction workers snored away.

Elsewhere, however, sailors were moving about the boat.

Zet thought about Princess Merit, hidden away somewhere. Were her kidnappers hurting her? Treating her how Kontar had treated him? The idea made him furious.

Glancing at the horizon, he watched the sun god, Ra, crest over the edge of the world. Feeling the warm rays on his skin, Zet closed his eyes and prayed.

Until I find her, keep Princess Merit safe!

"You have a funny look on your face," came Hui's voice.

Zet's eyes flew open. "Do I?" He grinned. "It's because my head's still ringing from you snoring in my ear all night."

Hui stretched. "Keeps the flies away."

"What's that? I think I've gone deaf."

Hui cupped his hands and shouted into Zet's ear. "Keeps the flies away!"

"In your mouth, more like," Zet said, imitating a snore that involved sucking down a large fly and swallowing it.

"Very funny." Hui stood and rubbed his belly. "What's for breakfast? I'm starved."

Zet's own stomach growled. Being on the river gave him an appetite. He leapt up. "I think I smell bread toasting. Come on. Race you!"

Together, they made their way on shore. Zet kept an eye out for Kontar, but the sailor was nowhere in sight. Neither was the Captain.

The cook handed out loaded plates. Fried goose eggs with golden yolks. Toasted bread, dripping with sweet honey. Roasted, shredded waterfowl that was deliciously greasy and melted in your mouth. A sailor's breakfast, through and through. Meant to feed men who labored hard all day.

Zet and Hui leaned back and groaned, deliciously full.

"I can't move," Hui said.

"Me neither," Zet said. "Which is bad, because I think the boat's leaving."

"What?" Hui cried, leaping to his feet.

"Kidding!"

"No, I think you're right! Come on!" Hui gasped.

They sprinted on board as the sailors prepared to push off.

The cabin door opened, and the Captain emerged along with Kontar. Kontar wore an angry expression. Zet craned to see inside the cabin before the door closed, but it was too dark in there. Both men were arguing in low voices. They didn't notice Zet watching.

He wondered if he could sneak into the cabin. What was so important in there? Why were they arguing? Could they be hiding the Princess in the cabin?

A sailor gave Zet a shove.

"Forward deck or aft deck—move it," the sailor barked. "No passengers mid-ship when we're under sail."

THE MORNING PASSED with no chance to investigate the cabin further. But there were plenty of things to distract him. A strong wind carried them swiftly north, the prow cutting knife-like through the glistening water. Zet and Hui sat with the breeze in their faces. Pelicans, herons and egrets played in the reeds by the banks. A crocodile surfaced, raced alongside, then swished its leathery tail and dove out of sight. Dragonflies dipped and glittered.

Onward they flew. Despite everything, Zet felt sure he'd never grow tired of this view. As morning wore into afternoon, however, the wind began to die.

The sail flapped noisily, sagging overhead.

Hot air descended. The Captain barked out orders. Sailors took up the oars. The boat began moving once again, but nowhere near the pace they'd made under sail. Everywhere, faces gleamed with sweat. Kontar pulled the lead oar, glaring at Zet through narrowed eyes.

Then, over it all, came an eerie chant.

Zet had forgotten about the priest. Now, without the wind to carry the priest's voice away, he could hear the man muttering. The rowers rowed in rhythm to his song—if it could be called a song. In the heavy heat, it sounded more like a death march.

"Creepy," Hui whispered.

Even the construction workers seemed spooked. They glanced at one another, exchanging uneasy looks.

Hours passed. The Captain shouted a command. They'd reached a small canal, which cut sideways off the Nile. The rowers leaned into their oars, pivoting the big boat. Zet watched, impressed, as they nosed it into the smaller canal. Lush greenery brushed the hull, surrounding the waterway on either side. The dip and splash of oars propelled them slowly up it.

They lost sight of the Nile as the canal snaked around a bend. There the canal widened again.

Zet and Hui stared out over the bow. Flies buzzed and swarmed. The air smelled of marsh reeds and verdant overgrowth. Ahead, far inland, desert hills rose steeply skyward, turning dark shades of blue and purple in the dusk.

Evening had fallen by the time the winding canal finally opened into a large, circular lake—a harbor, Zet realized. The lamps of bobbing boats glowed here and there. Some boats floated at anchor. Others were tied to watersteps against the shore. More lamps flickered on land, revealing a large, busy camp.

Hui whistled softly. "Look at this place."

"It's a small city."

Somehow he'd stupidly pictured Abydos as a tiny, quaint place, with a group of tight-knit workers that would be easy to investigate. Not this huge, sprawling camp! Way further off, he could see even more lights glowing. A second camp? No wonder the Queen Mother's people couldn't find the Princess. They needed a full-on military search, which was not an option given the kidnappers would retaliate by killing her on the spot.

Zet recalled the Queen Mother's despair, which she had so quickly hidden. He'd sworn to himself then that he'd find Princess Merit.

Now with Abydos spread before him that promise seemed like some childish wish. He'd been arrogant, picturing this as some big adventure. This was no adventure—a girl's life was at stake.

His heart slammed and his fingers tightened on the rail.

As for questions about what was in the Captain's cabin, and why the two men were arguing, he had no clue. The voyage was nearly over. Time was running out.

He watched the makeshift city grow ever closer as the Captain maneuvered their boat toward shore.

10

BROTHERS IN THE DARK

The boat hummed with commotion as sailors unfurled ropes and made ready to dock.

"Hui," Zet said in a low voice. "Whoever kidnapped the Princess has a lot to lose if they're caught. You know that, right?"

Hui glanced sideways, meeting Zet's eyes. "I do, now that you bring it up."

"They'd kill us in a flash."

"Right. I see what you mean," Hui said.

"You still with me?"

"All the way."

The Captain steered the boat into an open berth between a dozen other vessels. As they glided sideways against the watersteps, sailors tossed lines to men onshore. Everywhere, people moved and chattered in the flickering lamplight.

Zet's eyes swept left and right, searching for the temple. He expected to see pillars rising in the darkness, the shadows of colossal statues, dark and undefined, looming over vast temple grounds. All he saw were tents and people.

He smelled meat roasting and his stomach grumbled.

"I wonder where we're going to stay?" Hui said.

"I guess we'll find out when we talk to Senna, the architect."

Hopefully not with Jafar. He might have helped Zet, but Zet still didn't trust him. Jafar seemed to have his own agenda, and Zet had no idea what that agenda was.

Hui shouldered his pack. "Ready?"

Zet still needed to get his hidden scroll. But Kontar was leaned up against the captain's cabin door, as if making sure everyone cleared the deck before he did the same. Zet pulled Hui out of view.

"I need to grab our papers. But I don't see how, Kontar is watching like a jackal."

Hui cracked his knuckles. "Good thing I'm a fast runner." With that, Hui shouldered his bag and sauntered around the corner.

Zet risked a peek.

Hui reached Kontar's side. He crooked a finger at the sailor. The man frowned and bent closer. Hui cupped his hands and said something to him. The man's face turned a bloody shade of red. He lunged at Hui, but Hui danced out of the way.

Hui raised his right hand high. In it, he held Kontar's dagger.

"Fetch," Hui shouted, and sent it flying toward shore.

Zet could just see the dagger's point drive its way into the dirt. Then Hui and Kontar were running. With a roar that made Zet's hair stand on end, Kontar retrieved his prized possession and sprinted after Hui. *The man would kill him!*

Zet needed to act fast.

Quickly, he crouched and dug in the vegetable crate for his scroll.

"Are you still here?" came the Captain's voice.

Zet flinched.

He whipped around, expecting to meet the Captain's eyes. But the Captain was facing the gangplank, a good twenty steps away. Zet let out a soft breath, realizing the man was speaking to someone else. Heavy footsteps sounded on the swaying walkway. Someone was coming aboard.

Zet closed the crate's lid. Getting the scroll had to wait. He knew he should get back into the shadows as far as he could. But maybe he could learn something. He crouched lower.

"Still here? Of course I'm still here," came the jolly reply. "Exactly where you left me."

"I didn't leave you," the Captain said, sounding annoyed. "You do what you want. Like always. So don't pull me into it."

This caused a bark of laughter. "So I do. Good to see you too, brother."

"Why are you hanging around this camp?" the Captain said.

"I like it here."

"You like it when there's something to be had," the Captain said.

"You're always down on me, aren't you? My big, impressive, first-born brother. Once in a while, you could say something nice."

There was a heavy pause.

"I'm sorry," the Captain growled. "I'd like to see you settled, is all."

"Worried about your reputation is how I see it," the brother said.

Zet could feel the tension, even without seeing them.

"I offered you a sailor's position."

"Work for you? Forget it," came the younger brother's voice. "But I'd take another duck hunting trip. How about it? You and me, up to the marshes in your big boat? The camp's still buzzing about the last feast we supplied."

"Not this time. I have some troubles I have to get back and deal with. But Darius—" He lowered his voice, and Zet strained to hear. "What's the word on the Princess?"

Zet perked up, instantly alert.

"They're not going to find her," Darius said.

"Wipe that grin off your face. It's a good thing we were duck hunting when she was kidnapped, or I'd think you were involved."

"Me?"

"It's your kind of game, isn't it? Fast money?"

"Like you said," snarled Darius, "We were duck hunting. And this is what I get? Accusations? Some family reunion."

The Captain said nothing.

Darius laughed as if trying to ease the tension. "I hope you're not leaving without saying hi to Nan."

The Captain blew out a breath. "If I see her tonight, good. If not, give my little sister my regards."

"How about leaving me your rowboat 'till you get back?"

At this, Zet twisted toward the small boat several feet behind him. His hands went slick with fear. He tensed, preparing to bolt for new cover.

"Are you serious? Leave you my skiff?" The Captain let out an explosive snort. "It's always about what you can get out of me. Well, I've given you plenty. And it all ends up broken. I'm tired of playing father."

"As if you could."

"Get a life, Darius. And stay out of mine."

"Gladly."

Footsteps tromped down the gangway. Zet waited for the Captain to follow, but the man stayed on deck. Hui must be frantic by now, wondering what was going on. That is, if Kontar hadn't caught him—Hui could be hurt. What if the Captain didn't bother to go to dinner and stayed here all night?

Zet sank into a sitting position. At least he'd learned something. Whatever the Captain was hiding had nothing to do with the kidnapping. He could cross the Captain and Kontar off his suspect list. He realized he'd scored his first point. Unfortunately, it meant he was back to having no real suspects.

It seemed like forever, but finally the Captain made his way off the boat.

Zet yanked up the crate's lid. He dug deep, grabbed his scroll, and stuffed it in his pack. Then he stood and ran for shore, glad for the cover of darkness.

SENNA

A desert wind was blowing, kicking up sand. Zet glanced along the wharf, blinking in the dust, but saw no sign of Hui. Worry gripped him. The area was deserted. Hitching his pack over his shoulder, he hurried for the lights and noise.

A giant, dusty tent proved to be the mess area. He reached the flap and pulled it open.

Inside, there had to be a hundred workmen. Again, Zet felt overwhelmed at the thought of investigating so many people. They sat in makeshift circles on the ground. Everyone was eating and talking, and the noise was deafening.

Zet heard a familiar shout.

He spotted Hui, sitting beside Jafar. Relief washed over him. With them were construction workers from the boat, along with half a dozen unfamiliar faces.

"Over here!" Hui shouted, jumping up and waving his arms. "Come on, what took you so long?" His face was flushed, and he was grinning. So much for being worried. Clearly, Hui was having the time of his life.

A smile creased Zet's face, and again he felt glad to have Hui there.

Zet weaved through the crowd.

When he reached Hui, several men made room. Zet smiled and

thanked them, sinking down gratefully. Large bowls in the center of the group had clearly been piled with food but were now mostly empty. Zet grabbed a dish and scavenged what he could. He cursed himself for being delayed. He was starving. Two dates, a burnt bread crust and a few slices of zucchini would never fill him up.

"What did you say to Kontar?" Zet asked with a grin.

Hui looked impish. "Something about his mother and baboons."

Laughing, Zet made quick work of his meal. "Thanks. I guess we better check in with Senna."

Standing, he glanced both ways for Kontar. Even though the scary sailor was no longer a suspect, Zet was glad the man was leaving tomorrow. He took one final look and saw no sign of him. Kontar must have headed back to the ferry.

At the exit, a tall, narrow-faced man stopped Zet. "You are the new boy?"

"We just got here, if that's what you mean," Hui said.

The man looked from one to the other. "The architect informed me to expect only a single runner."

"I brought a friend," Zet said.

The man raised one thin brow. "Indeed. Follow me."

THE MAN, who informed them his name was Ari, led them back down to the wharf's edge. They passed the big boat Zet and Hui had arrived on, and several others.

Ahead, tied up near a statue of Ra, lay a small, sleek vessel. The boat was painted with curling designs in gold leaf. In the rear, a sun canopy with open sides roofed in the deck. Under the canopy, plump cushions lay scattered in an inviting, messy jumble. From there, a long, polished wood cabin stretched down the vessel's middle. Talk about luxurious.

"Here we are," Ari said, and motioned them up the walkway.

On deck, the ship smelled of oiled acacia. Here and there, glints of gold gleamed in the twinkling lamplight. A carved falcon's head guarded the cabin door.

Zet felt like everyone here must speak in hallowed whispers.

The illusion broke when the cabin door slammed open.

A scrawny, white-haired man stood on the threshold. His eyebrows jutted out like giant white feathers. His sparse hair was surprisingly long. It stood mostly on end, flying this way and that in the gentle breeze. With his skinny arms and legs and jutting belly, he looked like a scrawny water bird.

The man's face broke into a toothy smile. "What's the hold up, Ari?"

The man bowed. "Master, I came as quickly as . . ."

"Yes, yes." Senna waved a bony hand at Ari. "Never mind, they're here. Go away. No, on second thought, bring us refreshments. Chamomile tea, sweet cakes, almonds, whatever you can drum up from that stingy cook of mine."

"But the boys just ate!" Ari said.

The architect ignored him. He motioned to Zet and Hui, his tunic flapping around his limbs. "Come in. This breeze is giving me arthritis."

Zet and Hui glanced at one another. Zet struggled with a terrible desire to laugh, which he definitely did not want to do. He could see Hui felt the same, because Hui pressed his lips together and made a wide-eyed face.

The cabin was long, all shifting shadows and flickering light. Piles of scrolls lay everywhere. Some were filed neatly in holes in the wall, but most were heaped on low tables or overflowed from baskets. A desk held writing implements: cakes of ink, drawing brushes and tools. The white-haired man maneuvered between the chaos. He made his way to a low table, surrounded by cushions.

"This way," he called, sweeping the table's contents into an already full basket. "And close that door behind you!"

"Yes, sir," Zet said.

"And don't call me sir! I'm ancient enough already without being called sir. It's Senna. And if Ari tells you otherwise, ignore him. Stiff bird, that one."

Zet glanced back and saw Ari had returned.

"Master," Ari said, "I've roused the cook. She's taking care of your order."

Senna was easing himself onto a cushion. He looked up and beamed.

"Excellent! Probably complaining, too, the old tyrant. But I have to show some muscle once in awhile. Isn't that right, boys?"

"Er . . ." Zet said.

"Definitely," Hui agreed. "Tell her what's what!"

"My thoughts exactly," Senna said. "Wait. What's this? Two boys? Why am I seeing double?"

Ari said, "If there's anything else?"

"No, no, go away. Close the door," Senna said.

Zet said, "It's my fault. When the Queen Mother came to me for help, I asked if I could bring a friend. She agreed. This is Hui, and I'm Zet by the way."

The architect narrowed his eyes. "The Queen Mother, you say? Who said anything about the Queen Mother?"

THE PRIESTESS

In the dimly lit cabin Zet stared at Senna, thrown off guard. The dancing light made Senna's jutting brows look eerily like goat horns.

"I thought—" Zet began, and broke off.

Senna's eyes glittered, fixed on his face.

Zet swallowed. Was Senna testing him? "Wait." He dug through his pack and produced the tube. "Here, my papers."

Senna took the tube, opened the lid and tipped the scroll into his gnarled hand. He broke the seal and unrolled the document. He could read quickly, that was obvious. Under his strange exterior was an aura of intelligence. Maybe that's what made him a good architect—a crazy mix of wisdom and eccentricity.

Still looking at the page, Senna spoke in a non-committal voice. "Interesting."

"I also have this," Zet said, pulling the cord with the Queen Mother's ring from around his neck.

Hui gasped. "Where did you get that?"

A smile lit Senna's wrinkled features. "Well now. I'd say the chase is on!"

Zet blew out a huge sigh of relief. "Good. I hope it's okay if we get right to it? I have a lot of questions. Mostly, I want to know how Princess Meritamon disappeared. Wasn't she guarded?"

"Hush!" Senna said, waving his arms wildly. "Don't say her name!"

"Sorry," Zet said, wincing.

"Sound carries over water," Senna said.

"Who else knows besides us?" Hui asked.

"Ari, of course," Senna said. "Her closest servants, and one or two medjay. As for the rest of the medjay, they think they're searching for a priestess. So does everyone in the camp. And it's vital we keep it that way."

"What about the Captain of the boat we came here on?" Zet asked. "Does he know who she is?"

"Definitely not."

Zet frowned. His mind flashed back to the conversation he'd over-heard between the Captain and his brother. The Captain had asked about the *Princess*. But maybe Zet had heard wrong. Maybe he'd said *Priestess*. The words sounded similar, and they'd been whispering.

"Got something to say, spit it out," Senna said.

"It's nothing. Go on," Zet said.

At that moment, a ruddy-faced woman entered bearing a tray of delicious scented sweetmeats and a large cake. She set the tray down, left and returned with a steaming pot of tea. Then she fussed around, serving out generous slices of cake to Zet and Hui. Zet, who was starving, took his plate gratefully.

"Need some meat on those bones," she told him, her cheeks dimpling as he dug in.

"What about me?" Senna crowed.

She set a plate down in front of the scrawny architect. "You'll get indigestion eating this late."

"Oh good," Senna said. "Some excitement to look forward to."

She ignored him. To Zet and Hui, she said, "Try my glazed apricots. They're delicious."

"We will," they assured her as she bustled out the door, humming a tune.

"Indigestion, indeed," Senna said. "Now. Where were we?"

"You were telling us what happened when the . . . *Priestess* got here."

"Excellent. Yes. Thoroughness, that's what we need. A top to bottom telling of events. Let's see, she arrived by boat six days ago with half a dozen servants. She docked three boats down." He pointed to the wall, as if they could see through it. "I wanted her next to me, but others had arrived first, and since no one knew who she was, she couldn't claim precedence. But that's no matter." He waved his hand. "After she got settled, she came right here. A bright girl! And interested, too. We went over the drawings of her father's temple. She wanted to know what had been done, and what was still left to do. Of course, we're only early in the temple construction." He rambled on about columns and mud bricks, and how they'd moved blocks to the site for use, which had taken nearly a year in itself.

Zet finished his cake. Hoping it wouldn't be rude to take another slice, he did.

"But you don't want to hear about all that," Senna scolded, "Why are you letting me ramble?"

"Er—sorry!" Zet said, glancing at Hui.

"We're interested in all of it!" Hui cried. Being an artist, he clearly meant it.

Zet, however, did his best to shift topics. "Where was she kidnapped from? Her boat?"

"No." Senna took a long sip of tea. "Since you've just arrived, I should explain the layout here. To get to the temple, you must walk inland fifteen minutes. That's why I need a runner. I work from my boat. Doctor's orders." He toyed with his cake. "For three days in a row, she set out on a little mule to visit my construction site. The distance is too far for her."

"But it's only a fifteen minute walk," Zet said. Princess Merit, with her bright, laughing face, didn't seem like the type to insist on some old mule to get around.

"Why would she ride an old donkey?" Hui said.

Senna said, "How the healthy scorn the weak!"

"Weak? What's weak about her?"

Senna drummed his bony fingers. Then he cleared his throat. "Here's a little known secret, so keep it to yourselves. That bright young girl has a deformed spine. She was born with a back that curves like a disobedient old tree." He nodded, watching their faces. "Not only is she in continual pain, it affects her health greatly."

Zet's jaw dropped. "But that's—"

"Impossible!" Hui said, finishing Zet's thought.

"Oh, she takes great pains to hide it. You never see it in her face. She's livelier than anyone. Maybe that's why. She doesn't want people to know. And if you care for her, you'll keep it to yourselves. I only tell you for the sake of this investigation."

"You don't need to worry," Zet said. "Her secret's safe."

"So now you see why she went by mule."

"She must be in agony, wherever they're keeping her," Hui said, looking as furious as Zet felt.

"How long have they had her?" Zet said, fists clenched.

"Four days." Senna smoothed his brows with a shaking hand. "I told her to take more attendants. Stubborn girl. *A priestess is not surrounded by attendants, Senna. People will wonder!* Her words. She didn't take one man with her. Just two girls. I should have insisted."

Zet wanted to say it wasn't Senna's fault, but was it?

Senna stared at his barely touched piece of cake. He sighed and pushed it away.

13

CONSEQUENCES

Questions raced through Zet's head as he stared across the table at the architect.

"Where was she kidnapped from, exactly?"

"A partially constructed chapel."

"With so many workers, someone must have seen *something*," Hui said.

"We're not working on the chapel at present, and it backs onto unused land. Shrubs and tall grasses. It's easy to go there without being seen."

"Whose idea was it to go there?" Zet said.

"Hers, I assume."

Zet wasn't so sure. "What about her attendants? The girls? What happened to them?"

"One was kidnapped. The other's here."

"Here? How did she get away?" Zet said, stunned.

"By pure luck. The Priestess had sent the girl to investigate a loud crash. While the handmaiden was gone, the kidnappers moved in."

"A crash?"

"There was a construction accident. The girl returned to the chapel, found them missing and raised the alarm."

"And that was four days ago?

"Yes."

Zet rubbed his face. "Four days. She could be anywhere by now."

"Well, don't forget the ransom, and the agreement. If there's to be a handover, she can't be too far away."

"True."

Hui said, "What exactly do the Hyksos want?"

"They want Pharaoh to remove our army's blockade at Avaris. We're winning by preventing the Hyksos from getting reinforcements."

"How did the kidnappers even know the Priestess was you-know-who?"

"Khamudi, the rebel leader, must have spies here."

The cake in Zet's stomach felt heavy. "Would Pharaoh remove the blockade?"

"Canaan warriors would more than double the Hyksos army. We'd be sorely outnumbered. Everything we've fought for the last twenty years would be lost."

"Then that's not going to happen. We'll find her," Zet said.

"Don't make promises you can't keep." Senna unfolded his ancient limbs and got to his feet with a grimace. "It's late. Ari is constructing a tent for you boys. As to whether he's capable, I'll let you find out."

Zet still had questions, but it was obvious the interview was over.

He and Hui scrambled up.

"Be here first thing tomorrow," Senna said.

"Wait," Zet said, "I was wondering, what happened to your original runner? The one who worked for you before we got here?"

Senna put his bony fists on his hips. "Ill."

Zet frowned. "He's ill?"

"That's what I said. Now good night."

Outside, Hui said. "Ill? I don't believe it for a minute. What a strange thing to say."

"What do you think happened to him?"

Hui made a slicing motion across his throat.

"Don't be stupid," Zet said with a nervous laugh.

The cook appeared on deck and told them where to find Ari.

The tent was leaning ominously to one side when Zet and Hui

reached it. A roar came from inside. A long arm shot out, and then a foot, and then the whole thing tumbled into a heap.

"Flea dung!" shouted Ari from inside.

Zet and Hui hurried to rescue him. Ari appeared from the folds, his face red and his hair damp with sweat.

"Hey," said Hui. "Should be easy with three of us."

Fifteen minutes later, they stared at their lopsided creation scratching their heads.

"I thought you said this would be easy," Zet said.

"Yeah, well." Hui raised his shoulder, sheepish. "It's a roof. It's windy out here and calm in there. I'm beat, and I'm going to sleep."

"Good idea."

"Excellent idea," Ari said. "Allow me to bid you good night." The tall man bowed and made a hasty retreat. Clearly, he didn't want any more to do this evening.

Neither did Zet.

Yawning, he crawled inside with his pack. Bedding had been provided. Zet barely registered the soft coverings. He lay down, rested his head in the crook of his elbow, and dozed off.

The next morning, Zet woke later than planned. He shook Hui. "Wake up!"

Hui fought him off with a few slugs.

Ducking, Zet said. "Quit it, it's me!"

Hui rubbed his eyes. "So it is." He grinned. "Nothing like a bad dream to get me out of bed."

"Thanks. Speaking of bad dreams, you have drool on your face."

"Explains why I'm so thirsty," Hui replied. "I must have drooled myself dry."

"Gross." Zet grinned and crawled out of their crooked tent.

In broad daylight, the mysterious shadows of night had disappeared. He went still, taking in the spectacular view.

Rosy dawn splashed the circular bay with sparkles and streaks of colored light. The water undulated with soft movement. Boats rocked here and there. Their tie ropes, dripping with water, rose and fell with the creaking vessels. In the distant shallows, ibis birds poked around where the bay met a sandy shore.

"We're not in Thebes any more," Hui said.

"That's for sure." Zet's family and home seemed an impossible distance away. "I wonder how my mother and Kat are doing?"

"I wonder if Kat's still mad at me. Do you think she's still mad?"

"She's probably found another boy to crush on," Zet said.

Hui's mouth dropped open. "What? Really? No! Do you think so?"

Zet groaned. "It was a joke. Not to change the subject, but it's late. Let's split up—grab us breakfast and I'll find out what Senna wants us to do."

"Good idea," Hui said, rubbing his belly. "I'm starved." With that, he took off for the mess tent.

Back on board the architect's boat, Ari and Zet bid each other good morning.

"He's waiting for you," Ari said.

Zet crossed the sun-warmed planks and let himself through the door.

Senna sat at his desk, buried up to his elbows in scrolls. The old man looked up. He wore a beaded wig, which might have made him look more dignified. Except that the wig was slightly off kilter. His white brows were feather-like as ever, and shot up at the sight of Zet.

"There's no explanation for it," Senna said. "It's a waste!"

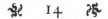

14

TROUBLE

Zet hovered in the architect's doorway. "Er . . . can I help, sir?"

He remembered belatedly that Senna asked him not to call him sir, but Senna seemed too distressed to notice.

"Not unless you can make me a new obelisk!" He glared at Zet. "It'll take weeks to bring a new stone here. And have it carved and . . . oh, never mind!" He waved a hand as if to bat the subject away.

Zet shuffled his feet. Finally, he said, "I came for my orders?"

"Of course you have." Senna scrubbed his forehead, shoving the wig further back. He blew out a sigh. "Can you draw?"

"Not well."

Senna's lips curled down. "That's unfortunate." He shuffled through the piles on his desk. Then he moved to the baskets. Finally, he pulled out a scroll, held it aloft and shouted, "Ha! Here it is. My original drawing plan. Well, don't just stand there with your mouth hanging, come!" Senna spread the scroll across the low table. "Hold that corner down."

Zet put his fist on it.

"Here," Senna said, tapping the drawing with a bony finger. "The spot where she disappeared. When I'm done, that chapel will house a great shrine, and only the High Priest will be allowed to enter."

"I'll go there right now," Zet said.

"Yes. Good. The medjay have searched it, of course, but it's best if you see the sight for yourself."

"Definitely. Can I take this with me?"

"Take it, mark it. Clues and all that. Anything unusual, mark it down for me. Then bring it back."

"All right." Zet doubted there would be any clues left at this point. What he wanted to do was start asking people questions. "What should I mark it with?"

Senna produced a stick of charcoal. "Can you manage with this?"

"I can't write, but I'll do my best."

"Good enough." Senna frowned, as if noticing something. "Where's your partner?"

"Fetching breakfast."

"Late rising, hey? Go outside and find Ari. He has your uniform. Get changed, drag your friend from the old feeding trough and have him report in."

"No disrespect, but I can tell Hui our instructions on our way to the site."

"Hui won't be joining you. I still need a proper runner. Hui's it."

Zet tried to mask his disappointment. He saw no point arguing. Hui could still ask questions while running messages to and fro, couldn't he? In fact, spread out, he and Hui could cover more ground.

On deck, Ari handed him a tunic with the architect's mark stitched across the chest and back. Over the tunic went a belt with loops and pouches. Zet buckled it and tucked the drawing plans into one loop. Then he went to find Hui.

There was no sign of him on shore. Zet headed for the mess tent, wondering what could have held him up.

"Let go of me!" shouted a voice.

"Hui," Zet groaned. What in the name of the gods was he up to?

He soon caught sight of the scuffle. Three medjay were jumping around a small, struggling figure. One medjay got a kick in the shins; another pinned the boy's arms back.

A crowd had formed. It grew larger by the minute. Zet sprinted toward them.

"Stop struggling!" shouted one medjay.

"I found it," Hui said fiercely. "Tell the stupid girl it was there already!"

The girl in question was probably Zet's age. Her thin arms clutched a large, leather bag. The bag was wet, and drops pooled at her beaded sandals. Clearly she didn't enjoy being called stupid. Her cheeks were red, offsetting the deep black color of her hair. Her eyes were striking, large and lined with kohl. Despite her anger, she was very pretty.

"He was stealing them!" she shouted. "He's a thief!"

"I am not a thief!" Hui shouted back.

"Then what were you doing with this bag?"

"Don't worry, miss," a medjay said, fastening Hui's wrists with rope. "He'll be dealt with."

Zet stared, stunned as the medjay hauled Hui off. Hui kept struggling and hadn't spotted Zet in the crowd.

Flea dung! This was the last thing they needed.

"What happened?" Zet demanded, turning to face the scowling girl.

Her flashing eyes raked over him. "It's none of your business."

Hui might be a joker, but he would never steal someone's stupid bag. The idea was ridiculous. Not that she'd understand.

"We both work for the architect. I'll have to explain to my boss why he's lost a runner. Could you please at least give me an idea of what happened?"

Patches of color appeared in her cheeks. "I found him crouched along the river, holding the bag."

"Maybe he was just washing his hands?"

She put her fists on her slim hips and leaned forward. "He wasn't. I saw him with it!"

"Maybe he found it?"

"Found it?" Her cheeks flushed deeper and she stomped her foot. "Just like a boy to not believe me! He was tying the bag to a branch so it wouldn't float away. I caught him doing it! I saw him! Do you have any idea of the value of what's in here? No, of course you don't. That's why you don't understand."

"You're right, I don't," he said stiffly so as not to laugh. Which was ridiculous, because this was horribly serious. She reminded him of his favorite cat, clutching some feline prize.

She held the bag tighter. "They're my mistress's jewels."

"Jewels?" His throat constricted. "Uh, and who, exactly, is your mistress?"

"The Priestess who was kidnapped four days ago."

Zet felt like he'd been crushed flat by a giant boulder. This girl was Princess Merit's handmaiden. And Hui had been found with a bag of royal jewels.

"This is terrible," he choked out.

She sat down on a weathered stone. "You have no idea."

Zet sank down beside her. "Why, by the toes of Bastet, did she bring something so valuable here?"

It was more of a lament than an actual question. The girl, however, said, "She wanted to wear them to a special event. After we left."

Zet nodded, thinking that one minute the Princess had been looking forward to her fourteenth birthday party, and the next she was caged in some horrible place, wondering if she was going to die.

The girl sighed. "Sometimes life has a way of taking us by surprise," she said quietly.

He followed her gaze across the lush soil and into the dry hills beyond. The swaying palms marked the edge of the humid earth. Once you passed those shady guardians, the world became all blinding heat. A waterless desert filled with deadly scorpions, snakes, hyenas and lions, waiting to claim your life. If thirst didn't kill you first.

Where could they have taken the princess?

"Is there any news from the medjay? They're looking for her, aren't they?" he said.

"Yes. Not that it's done any good."

"I'm sorry," he said, realizing she and Princess Merit must be close friends.

She said, "Without that runner, will you have to do double the work?"

Hui. He had to get Hui free. They'd have to let him go!

She watched his face. "It's good the boy was caught."

"Well—"

"You don't want to be working with a thief, do you?"

"Right. I mean, no." Zet felt horrible at pretending Hui was a thief. He couldn't tell her Hui was his best friend. She seemed nice and he hated deceiving her, but he had a job to do. This was an opportunity to find out first hand what happened to the Princess. Anyway, she wanted the same thing, right?

"I guess I better go," she said.

Seeing his chance slipping away, he blurted, "Look, I'm just a messenger boy, but I want to help find your priestess."

She stiffened. "I don't see how you could."

"I don't know either."

Her shoulders relaxed and she sighed. "Thanks for offering."

"What's your name?"

"Naunet. What's yours, messenger boy?"

"Zet."

"Well, Zet, I have to go put this away." She rose. "Perhaps I'll see you again."

He sat there dumbly, watching her flit off like a little bird with her white dress fanning out behind and wondered why he enjoyed hearing her say his name so much.

Speaking of names, why did hers sound so familiar? *Naunet.* Had the Queen Mother mentioned it? No. Nothing came to him.

Hui flashed into his mind and he felt suddenly sick.

How were they going to get out of this?

It was time to go help Hui. Zet ran in the direction the medjay had taken him.

15

ARRESTED

Blue sky arched overhead, rich as royal turquoise. Palm fronds cast jagged shadows over the warm earth underfoot. A scorpion scuttled across Zet's path, its tail curved in the familiar, deadly arch. Zet skidded to a halt. The creature paid him no notice. It went on its way, scuffling into the dry grass. If Zet had been running any faster, he'd have stepped on it. Probably puncturing his foot in the process.

He could be brave about a lot of things, but poison wasn't one of them. What a horrible, terrifying death that would be. He shuddered.

From now on, he'd have to be more careful where he stepped out here.

Moments later, he spotted Hui far along the wharf. Shoulders sunburnt after their two days on the boat, Hui sat on a stone block looking sullen. Two medjay stood there, one on either side. Behind them, an official medjay police boat was tied up securely. The medjay's symbol was painted on its hull and sewn into a flag that fluttered atop the mast.

Hui glanced up as Zet neared. His eyes brightened and he scrambled to his feet.

"Sit down!" one medjay barked.

Hui sat. He crossed his arms, grumbling about stuck up girls who were too stupid to see he was telling the truth.

Nerves clenched Zet's belly. "I'm sure we can explain this. It was just a big mistake."

"And who might you be?" one medjay asked.

"We work together."

"Not anymore. Now clear off."

Zet's hands were sweating. "If you come with me and talk to our boss—"

"I'll do no such thing!" roared the closest medjay. "This is official business. If you don't leave immediately, I'll arrest you too."

"But sir—"

"And still you keep talking! One more word and I swear you'll be thrown in shackles for the rest of your short life."

Hui leaped to his feet. "You have no right!"

The medjay grabbed Hui, and was about to deal him a heavy blow when a deep voice boomed, "What's all this, then?"

"Commander, you're here, thank the gods," said the nearest medjay.

He snorted. "You called me back to deal with two boys?"

Zet stared at the commander's face in disbelief. As of yet, the commander hadn't looked at him. The man stood taller than the rest. His chest was broad and muscled, and he had hands the size of platters. A wide belt circled his muscled midsection, and a sword hung from a loop. His brows were thick, and his square jaw was shadowed with a faint hint of stubble. He turned his eyes on Zet. His mouth opened in surprise.

"Zet?" he said in disbelief.

Zet grinned, so glad to see his old friend Merimose that he wanted to shout with joy.

Merimose shifted to squint at Hui. His disbelief turned to outrage. "Hui, too? By every god, what in Ra's name are you boys doing here?"

Despite the big man's tone, Zet felt relieved. He and Merimose had had their share of run-ins back in Thebes—most of them good. Even if Merimose did have a way of forgetting how helpful Zet had been in past cases, he'd get Hui free. Zet felt sure of it.

To the men, Merimose said. "You're dismissed." To Zet and Hui, he said, "On board. Both of you. We need to have a little chat."

The nearest medjay protested. "Commander, I'd like to report what this boy was doing."

"I'll get a full explanation. Don't you worry." He glared at Zet and Hui.

The medjay shrugged. Then, with fresh orders from Merimose, he and the other man marched off with their weapons jingling at their sides.

This was the third boat Zet had been on in as many days. It was as different as the other two. Everything about it seemed ship-shape and official. More sparkling clean than his mother's kitchen, the deck practically squeaked underfoot. Merimose ushered them into the central cabin. It was like a miniature version of the office in Thebes. Cubbyholes held neatly rolled scrolls. The place gleamed with efficiency. At present, it was empty.

Merimose shut the door.

"Explain yourselves," he growled.

Zet and Hui started in at once, both talking over each other.

"Stop!" Merimose said, raising a hand. "Zet, you first. Don't you have a pottery stall to run? If I hear you've come because—no, that's not possible. No one knows except myself and a few others." He rubbed his head. "Why are you here?"

"Well . . . " Zet began. "It's not true, exactly, that no one knows about—"

"This is outrageous!" Merimose said. "If you tell me you're here because of some rhino-brained idea that you're an investigator . . . oh, by the beard of Osiris, I can read it in your face! That *is* why you're here. How did you possibly find out? Of all the ridiculous things a boy could do!"

"It wasn't my idea," Zet said quickly. He glanced at Hui for help.

Hui's mouth dropped open. "Don't look at me, I'm in enough trouble."

"Yes," Merimose said drily. "We'll get to that."

"Look." Zet lowered his voice to a whisper. "The Queen Mother came to me. She figured I could help, just ask questions, that's all."

"She did, did she?"

"I'll prove it!" Zet pulled out the Queen Mother's ring.

Merimose waved his huge right hand. "Put it away. Whatever you might be, you're not a liar. Not about something like that. But Queen Mother or not, I can't have you running all over, upsetting my investigation and getting underfoot!"

"We're working for the architect as runners. We won't be!"

Merimose rubbed his face and sighed. "You already are. Want to explain what happened out there?"

Hui said, "It was a simple mix up. Honest. I'm making a lock, and I needed a piece of wood to make a pin. I saw the bush along the river's edge, and was going to cut off a piece. There was a rope dangling from the bush into the water. I was curious, so I pulled on it, the bag came up, and then that girl showed up and started screaming at me. I didn't even know that some jewels were in there until later!"

Merimose said, "You found a bag of jewels? Great. Just great. Who was the girl?"

"Naunet is her name," Zet said.

Hui glanced at him like he was a traitor. "You talked to her?"

"Naunet?" Merimose said. "It gets even better! Not only did you find jewels, they're royal jewels."

Zet and Hui were silent. Zet didn't like the look on Merimose's face.

"I can't let you go, Hui. I'm going to have to lock you up."

"What?" Hui gasped. "But I'm innocent!"

Merimose grimaced. "I believe you. But others won't. You'll have to stand trial."

"Stand trial?" Hui blanched. "Are you serious?"

"Unless we find out who put that bag in the river, I'm afraid I am."

Sweat broke out on Zet's forehead. "You're the Commander, the head medjay."

"Yes. Which means I have to uphold the law. I'm sorry boys, my hands are tied."

"This can't be happening." Zet stared at Hui's pale face. "Don't worry. There's no way I'm letting you stand trial. I brought you here. I'm going to find out who did this."

"No," Merimose said. "You're going to leave things to me and my men."

Zet's mouth opened. He glared at the commander.

"If you want to keep working for the architect, I can't stop you. As for this case, drop it. If you start poking around, you put not only you, me and my men at danger, you might get the Princess killed."

Hands in fists, Zet stared at the scrubbed wooden floor.

"Do you understand me?" Merimose asked.

Zet nodded.

"I mean it. These people are vicious. They've kidnapped *Pharaoh's* daughter. They plan on winning their battle against Egypt with this move. If they suspect you're snooping around, you're dead." He paused. "And as for that ring you're wearing? I advise you to find a spot and bury it. One look and they'll know you're the Queen Mother's spy."

Hui shot Zet a frightened look.

"It's time you went back to shore," Merimose said.

16

A PRIEST'S WORK

Z et stood on the wharf, wondering how things had turned so badly.

Hui was going to have to face trial. If they found him guilty, he'd be put to death. The image was so bleak, his legs felt numb. He sat heavily on a stone block and stared blankly ahead.

Hui, dead?

Zet couldn't give in to panic. If he did, Hui would be lost for certain.

He tried to summon his courage. There was only one way to save him. Unravel the mystery, fast.

Back at Senna's boat, he gave Ari the news. Then he left quickly. Back on shore, Zet's skin prickled with a sense of being watched. He glanced at the gently rocking boats, but saw no one. His fingers went to the ring hidden on the chain around his neck.

He needed to hide it, but not in broad daylight. He'd wait until night.

His stomach grumbled loudly. He cursed at it, but knew he needed food. He took one last glance at the medjays' boat. Then he skirted by the dining tent like a dog looking for stray scraps.

"Meal's over!" said a woman clearing away the last of the empty platters.

"I don't suppose you have leftovers? I missed it."

"Wake up earlier, next time!"

He went outside. Behind the tent lay the cooking area with a giant fire pit and huge pots for making meals to feed a crowd. He spotted a basket with a heel of bread. It would have to do.

"Oho, no you don't!" shouted the cook. "You're the one whose been nibbling at my stores! You already got a cooked meat pie last night!"

"That wasn't me," Zet said.

She relented. "All right then. Can't have you fainting. Grab a handful of dates while you're at it. In the sack behind the beer jug."

He grabbed the bread and dates. "Thank you!"

He headed for the temple in the distance, chewing as he went.

"Boy, hey!" came a man's voice. "You there, stop!"

Zet turned. It was the priest from the boat. The man stood in the shade of a palm tree. His linen kilt was so white it was nearly blinding. How did he manage to keep it so clean in a place like this?

"Hurry," the priest said. "How dare you keep me waiting?"

Zet frowned. "Whoever you're waiting for, it's not me. I'm on business for the architect. And I have to get going."

The priest eyed Zet sharply. "The architect's business can wait. I am the High Priest of Osiris. You will do my bidding."

At this, Zet gulped. High Priest to Osiris, God of the Underworld? So that's why the man had such dark energy. A chill ran down Zet's spine. He definitely didn't want to risk stirring up the wrath of the mighty God of the Dead.

"What do you need me to do?" Zet asked.

The priest motioned to the large wooden chest at his feet. The sides were inlaid with gold and jewels. The top looked extremely strange, like it was made out of the wings of some large bird. A falcon perhaps.

"Carry this and follow me," the priest said. He set off in the direction of the half-constructed temple of Pharaoh Ahmose.

Zet hurried to get the rectangular box. He had to stretch his arms wide to grasp the rope handles on either end. It took two tries to heft it off the ground. Now, with the strange feather lid so close to his face, he saw that it was definitely wings. Four of them, all stitched together and held in place with leather hinges on one side.

Chills rippled along Zet's forearms where they touched the thing. Eerie.

What was in there that was so heavy? Zet was wiry, but strong for his size given that he spent most days hefting heavy pottery jugs, urns and stacks of plates around his stall back home. Lean muscles stood out on his arms. He tightened his handhold and hurried to catch up.

"I guess you know about the missing priestess?"

The man didn't answer.

A thought struck. "Wait, is that why you've come?"

The man walked faster.

Was it possible the Queen Mother had sent the priest, too? If so, they were working for the same cause. "Are you here to help?"

The priest paused. "Her disappearance has placed a stain on this holy ground."

What was that supposed to mean? It wasn't her fault she was kidnapped.

The priest sped up.

Zet decided to try again. "The architect asked me to go to the chapel where she was taken. He wants to start building there soon. I know it's none of my business, but I was thinking—maybe you want to come with me? Being a holy man, you'd be able to spot anything out of place."

The priest turned and snapped, "The matter has nothing to do with you. Remember your place, serving boy."

Zet felt his cheeks turn hot.

He swallowed, thinking of the Queen Mother who'd sent him with so much trust. He had no business trying to solve this case! What was he doing here? Everything was all messed up.

Time was slipping away. Hui was facing a death trial. Zet had learned nothing about the Princess's hostage location. Pharaoh would be here in a few days. Panic rose and he shoved it down.

The priest began to chant. More like a stream of low sounds than actual words. He marched to the creepy tune.

In Zet's arms, the box shuddered of its own accord. His eyes flicked to the priest, and back to the flimsy feather lid. Sweat stood out on his chest and arms.

What was in there?

Ahead, stone pillars and half built walls rose to the sky. They were nearing the construction site. Men moved in teams, building, carving, painting. Before Zet could breathe a sigh of relief, however, the priest kept going.

Whatever was inside the box shifted again.

Zet kept his eyes on the lid, trying to see between the feathers.

"Stop and kneel," the priest said.

"What?" Zet glanced up. He'd been so focused on the chest he hadn't noticed anything else.

He sucked in a shocked breath.

He stood at the base of a huge triangle. The building tapered in and up on all four sides, and came to a single point on top. A pyramid! He'd heard of such things, but never dreamed he'd see one. The angled walls shone in the sunlight, so smooth you wanted to run up to them and glide your hand over the surface.

Instead, Zet set the chest down and sank to his knees.

"This will be the burial place of Pharaoh," the priest said. "If you value your life and your health, you will pray now to be forgiven for setting your eyes upon it."

Zet never asked to set his eyes upon it. Still, he thought it best to take the High Priest's advice, and whispered every fervent prayer he could think of.

17

THE BOX

"Now," the priest said, rising, "Attend me to the entrance."

Zet rose, hefted the box up again and headed for the pyramid's arched entryway.

"That is a false door. Only spirits may pass through it."

The priest marched around the pyramid's far side. Zet struggled after him with the monstrous box. When he rounded the corner, he spotted several medjay. They stood guard at the entrance to the giant structure. Something about this suddenly felt very official. The medjay were obviously waiting.

Was it because they needed to get inside, but didn't dare?

Zet gasped. "Do you think the kidnappers are hiding the priestess in there?" He was horrified, but saw how it could make a good hiding spot. No Egyptian would risk the curses for entering the pyramid. Maybe the Hyksos believed they were immune to the wrath of Egypt's gods.

"We shall see."

At the entrance, the medjay gave the priest a wide berth. Even they seemed to fear his spooky presence. A sudden tune issued from the priest's lips. It echoed sharply off the hot, slanted wall. It rose to an alarming pitch.

Zet felt his cargo thrash. Jarred by the terrifying movement, he carefully lowered the box to the ground.

As he did, the feather lid began to rise.

Startled, he crouched motionless.

The lid continued to open. A sleek, scale-covered head snaked up from the opening. The serpent's body moved and writhed, pushing itself higher, weaving back and forth. Its eyes were like glass, black and shining. Zet stared into its cold, hypnotizing gaze.

Clammy terror made his insides turn to liquid. A king cobra.

The cobra's hood opened, wide and muscled. Its colored patterns dazzled him. With a hiss, the serpent's tongue flicked out. Gaze fixed on Zet's gaping face, it reared back, revealing dagger-like fangs.

Death had come.

In a flash, the cobra shot forward.

Zet rolled onto one shoulder and tumbled away. As he scrambled to get clear, he flinched, waiting for the bite.

He heard the snake come at him through the dirt and he twisted in horror.

Then the priest was there, his hand snapping forward to catch the snake from behind. The man's sinewy fingers closed just below the cobra's head. He pulled it to his chest as if it were a pet. Meanwhile the snake hissed and spat, eyes glued to Zet.

"We have work to do," the priest told it. He turned and entered the pyramid, leaving Zet gasping in the dust.

"That was close," called one of the medjay.

Zet's heart was practically banging out of his chest. "He had me carry that box from the harbor! The lid wasn't even fastened."

"Ha! I wouldn't want to get on his bad side."

The second medjay laughed. "If we hear shouts from inside, we'll know someone has."

"Let's just hope he doesn't kill the missing priestess by mistake," said the first.

"He'd better not," Zet said in a harsh voice. Would the cobra know the difference between friend and foe? What if it killed the Princess in her father's own burial tomb? But the priest wouldn't be so careless. Would he?

Then again, the priest had called her disappearance *a stain on this holy ground.*

Zet thought back to a time in Thebes when he'd had a run in with the High Priest of Amenemopet. Not every man was who he seemed. Not everyone could be trusted. He hoped for the Princess's sake that this man was on her side.

He stood for a long time with the two medjay, but no sounds came from inside.

"Don't you have work to do, messenger boy?" a medjay asked.

With no excuse, he had to agree. He bid them goodbye and set off for the temple construction site. As he drew near, the sounds of ringing hammers against stone filled the air. The maze of half built walls looked daunting. Everywhere, men chanted in rhythm as they worked. Some were dragging a heavy stone into place. Farther off, a tall young man led a pair of donkeys weighted down with sacks of supplies. In a wide-open area, dozens of men were bending and scooping a muddy, wet substance into molds. Brick-makers, Zet realized.

He paused on the path and pulled out the architect's scroll. Time to find the partially built chapel.

Zet studied the complex drawing. He wished Hui were here to help make sense of it! The thought of his best friend sent fresh worry coursing through him. Zet had to figure out who'd stolen those jewels.

A thought struck. *Was it possible the kidnapping and the jewel theft were connected?*

He pondered this for some time. If there was an enemy spy in the camp like Senna suggested, that spy knew the Princess. He'd be close enough to steal her jewels. And if Zet found him, he'd save Hui and Princess Meritamon in one blow.

No more time to wait. He had to find that chapel. Studying the scroll, he tried to puzzle out the diagram. The lines had to be walls. And the breaks? Maybe they were doors? But what about the circles, and those small squares?

Finally, he just started walking.

Senna said the chapel was on the outer edge. Zet walked the work-site's perimeter. Glancing through the labyrinth of walls, he saw pillars and pylons reaching skyward. Heavy foliage forced him to turn into the site. He came across a wall painted end-to-end with a giant war scene. The mural showed Pharaoh leading his men against the Hyksos invaders. There were thousands of soldiers.

One had to be Zet's own father. Even though the faces were small and only representations of the fighting men, Zet reached out and ran his fingers over them.

"Come home safe," he whispered.

Footsteps sounded nearby. He glimpsed a medjay and started walking, quickly. He didn't want to rouse any suspicions, especially if Merimose was on site. Merimose would demand to know what he was doing. Friend or not the Commander would put a stop to Zet's investigation if he caught him disobeying his direct orders to do so.

He spotted a doorway barred off by a length of dusty fabric. The fabric was marked with the medjay's official symbol.

This was it. The site where the kidnapping had taken place.

Zet gulped and glanced around. Now or never. He raised the linen strip and ducked under.

The chapel was long and narrow. There was no roof yet, so the dirt floor was a mix of shadow and hot sunshine. Someday, this would all be decorated with spells and elaborate carvings. Even without them, it felt strange to be inside. Not just because the Princess had been kidnapped here. A mystical power seemed to grip the room with breathless silence.

Carefully, he combed the space for clues, all the while glancing back at the door.

Unfortunately, there wasn't much to see. A few dusty footprints, but that was all.

He should have figured as much.

Zet rubbed his head and blew out a frustrated breath.

18

THE SECRET WADI

Zet peered into the undergrowth that led away from the chapel.

The medjay must have searched for tracks. Still, it wouldn't hurt to take another quick look. He couldn't think what else to do, and time was running out.

Low scratchy bushes raked his shins. He zigzagged through them, searching for footprints or donkey hoofmarks.

Nothing.

He crouched in the shade of some waving bulrushes and pulled out the temple plans. Should he keep going?

Senna had shown him where the chapel lay. Now Zet began to understand the drawing better. He rotated it until the chapel on the page matched the chapel in the distance. Senna had only sketched a bit of the grassy area where Zet sat now.

He tried to think like the kidnappers. Which way would they go?

There were several choices. Hide here until dark, and then circle the temple perimeter, enter the mountains and hole up in a cave. It would be nearly impossible to find them.

But if they hadn't? If they'd gone straight away from the worksite, where would that take them? Zet decided to keep walking. Maybe he'd be lucky. Maybe he'd find a clue the medjay overlooked.

Standing, he glanced both ways. If someone spotted him—medjay or kidnappers—he'd be in trouble. A runner had no business combing the area for clues. As far as he could tell, no one was watching.

Stuffing the scroll in his waistband, he set off.

The scruffy bushes grew thicker the further he walked. Soon the undergrowth grew so thick that he had to stop and choose a new route. Backing up, he found a clearer way and kept going.

He was ready to give up when he noticed something. A bush crushed on one side. His heart began to race. He ran forward and discovered that the ground ahead sloped into a wadi, a marshy gorge.

He clambered down and slipped on fresh mud. When he landed on his butt, he nearly whooped at what he saw.

Hoofmarks.

There were hoofmarks! Fresh ones. A donkey had come through here. A number of them, by the look of it. *Was this the way they'd come?*

The wadi grew wider and deeper and the bluffs rose higher. Anyone could be up there and he wouldn't see them until it was too late. A wind whooshed over him, rattling dry bushes that clung to the slopes.

He began to run.

Feeling alone and exposed, he forced himself to keep going. How he wished Hui were with him. Glancing this way and that, he wound downward.

A forest of gnarled brush blocked the gulch's far end. Carefully, he approached. Holding his breath, he pried the brush apart. He had no idea what he expected to see. A hut perhaps, surrounded by guards. A cave with a guarded entryway. But he saw none of those things.

He stared in disbelief.

It was the canal.

The wadi had led him to the canal that ran between the Nile and Abydos harbor.

Disappointment flooded through him. All hope gone, Zet shoved his way through the bushes and out onto the red, sandy bank. He ran a hand over his head. He'd been so certain he was on the right track. This was nothing but a dead end.

His shoulders sagged. Finally, he turned and plodded back the way he'd come.

The hike seemed harder now. It seemed to take forever.

By the time he reached the worksite, his stomach was making fierce complaints. Judging by the sun's angle, noon and lunch had long since passed. Feeling hollow, he pushed through the last of the undergrowth.

As he emerged in front of the chapel, a man shouted at him.

"Hey! What do you think you're doing?"

Zet stood frozen, startled by the man's angry tone.

Two huge workers thrust their way toward him. The men were bare to the waist. Stone dust colored their skin, blending with their sweat. One wore leather wrist-guards that came halfway to his elbows. They made his bulging forearms look impossibly huge. The other had a soft belly, as if he'd only been doing construction for a short time. His arms were lean and patchy with fresh sunburns.

One grabbed Zet by his arm and dragged him toward the chapel.

"What's going on?" Zet said, glancing around for help. Now, when he actually wanted to see a medjay, none were in sight. His heart drummed in panic.

"Shut up." The guard thrust Zet under the linen that blocked the chapel door.

Zet sprawled in the dirt. He flipped over and leaped up as the two men followed him inside.

"What were you doing out there?" asked the sunburnt man. His voice was strangely familiar.

"I work for the architect," Zet said, stumbling back.

They kept coming at him until he was pressed against the wall.

"Out in the bushes?" The sunburnt man laughed. "What kind of work do you do in the bushes?"

"None! I came to check on the chapel," Zet said quickly. "He asked me to look for damage, and, well, I drank a lot of tea this morning. When I got here, I had to go. You know, nature calls." He swallowed and tried to look defiant. "Is there a crime against it?"

The sunburnt man eyed him closely. "The architect's a dangerous man to work for."

"Oh yeah?" Zet said. "Why's that?"

"Look what happened to his last runner-boy who came snooping."

Zet shrugged, although he felt sick with fear. "I got his job, that's all I care about."

"Is that so?"

"Why, what happened to him?" Zet asked.

The sunburnt man leaned down, right into Zet's face. His breath stank. "A horrible curse."

A warning told Zet to keep silent. Instead, he wrinkled his nose and said, "Did this curse have your name on it?"

The sunburnt man went still as death.

Big mistake, Zet decided. The Queen Mother's seal ring suddenly felt heavy against his chest. Merimose's warning came to him. He stared into the sunburnt man's eyes, wondering if he was staring into the face of Princess Merit's kidnapper. If they found it he was dead.

He needed to backtrack, fast.

Clenching his fists, he dropped his gaze to the ground. "Sorry," he muttered. "It's just, I'm new here, and I've been getting flack all day from my master."

He could feel their eyes drilling into the top of his skull.

"Hey! What's all this?" came a man's voice from the door.

All three turned. A man stood there, hands on his hips. He wore a medallion on one shoulder, and looked official. "What are you men doing? Get back to work."

The sunburnt man took a step back from Zet. Muscles worked in his jaw. "Watch yourself, boy," he said quietly

The thugs left. Zet followed. At the door, the official stopped him.

"This area is off limits. Why are you here?"

"The architect sent me," Zet said.

"I'm the Overseer—if he wants to send his servants poking around, he'd better talk to me first. Got it? Or maybe you want to talk to the medjay."

"No! No—I'm going."

19

THE PRISONER

B ack outside, Zet's heart was still racing. *What was that about?* He looked both ways. The two men were gone.

Was it possible they were Princess Merit's kidnappers? What other explanation could there be? And why were they worried about him snooping in the bushes? All he'd found was a dead end. If they'd taken the Princess that way, they'd put her in a boat and had sailed off where no one could follow. Everyone knew it was impossible to track a boat, so why would the two men be worried about him being in the brush?

Even more puzzling, why did the sunburnt man's voice seem so familiar? Where had Zet heard it before?

Part of him wanted to report his attackers to Merimose. But if Merimose questioned the men, they could deny it. They could say they caught Zet snooping. Merimose would be furious. Worse.

He could send Zet home.

The chilling realization shook him to his core.

Stumped, he headed back toward the harbor. It was time he checked in with Senna.

Small birds wheeled in the cloudless sky. Zet reached the road. He felt eyes on his back and turned. At the temple, hundreds of men still labored under the waning sun. He squinted, but saw no sign of his attackers. The sunburnt man's warning flashed through his mind—that the last runner had suffered a 'curse'.

Zet gulped, picturing a deadly visit from them to his tent in the middle of the night.

Hopefully, they believed what he told them—that he was just a clueless messenger.

His mind roamed to Hui, and his spirits sank even further. Nearly a whole day had passed, and what had Zet learned? Nothing. Fear for his best friend gnawed at him.

He felt dizzy, and realized it was more than fear. He'd eaten nothing since his meager breakfast, and the day was nearly over.

Deciding to risk the cook's anger, he angled off the road so he could come up behind the mess tent. Maybe he could beg a few scraps before dinner.

The smell of animal dung drifted on the soft breeze. He looked right and saw donkeys clustered in an open-air pen. Next to the donkeys lay a long, low, mud-brick building. A barn. Zet thought of the wadi and the donkey prints.

This was worth investigating.

As he neared the mud-brick building, a man stepped out. The man shielded his eyes from the slanting sun and watched Zet approach. His gnarled hands were calloused and stained with dirt. Straw dusted his tunic. He held a grooming brush. The stable master.

The man eyed Zet's uniform. "You're the other runner."

"The architect's runner? Yes."

"I suppose you've come to talk to the prisoner?"

Zet tried to hide his surprise. He glanced at the building. This is where they were holding Hui? "Yes," he said quickly. "Er, the architect wanted me to ask him something."

The man nodded. "Go in. Stall at the end. But don't be long."

Zet could hardly believe his luck! Until that moment, he didn't realize how completely alone he'd felt. Hui was here. They'd think of a plan out of this mess together.

It was dark inside. He squinted and made out a narrow pathway with animal stalls on either side. No doubt at night the stable master herded the donkeys in here to protect them from prowling lions and hyenas. The sound of soft breathing came from his right. He approached a stall door made of sturdy bamboo rods, and peered through.

Expecting to see Hui, he jolted in shock.

The figure curled on the ground, eyes closed, was a woman! Around his mother's age. The sight made him uncomfortable. Why was she locked up in here? He wrapped his fingers around the bars, working up the courage to wake her. He had to know.

Someone was coming. Zet wrenched himself away.

A tall man clad in pristine white robes appeared out of the gloom. He smelled of incense and temple oils. The priest.

"Hello," Zet said.

"Good evening." The priest kept walking, and soon disappeared.

How strange!

When Zet finally found Hui's stall, his best friend leaped up with a shout of joy.

"Tell me you've come to let me out."

"I wish," Zet said.

Hui's shoulders sagged. He pressed his forehead to the bamboo rods in despair.

"But I'm going to get you out," Zet said. "I swear it." They stood a moment in shared fright. "Are those your tools? And that lock you were carving? They let you bring those in here?"

Hui nodded. "Yes, the priest ordered them to."

"That priest? He almost killed me. What does he want from you?"

"Never mind that. What's important is that I'm going to break out." He pointed to the wall behind him. "I've been digging out the mortar between the bricks. It's slow work, but if you went around back of this place, you could help from the other side!"

"And then what, run for the rest of your life? It's like saying you're guilty."

"Either way, I'm dead."

"I told you I'm going to get you out."

"How?"

"Listen, the thief had to be a Hyksos spy. All I have to do is find him and unmask him for who he is."

Hui went silent. Finally, he said, "Do you have any leads?"

"Maybe." Zet told him about the hoofmarks in the wadi. And the attack in the chapel.

"Sounds like they're protecting something. But what?" Hui said.

"I don't know."

"Remind me what Senna said about that day. What time did she disappear?"

"I'm not sure. But I just thought of something. Remember that accident the girl went off to investigate? You know, when she left the chapel and came back to find it empty? Well, this morning Senna was in a horrible mood because of some obelisk that fell over at the worksite. That must have been the accident. I wonder if it's important to the mystery?"

Hui's eyes lit up. "It might be. I heard people talking about it at breakfast!"

"What did they say?"

"Some men told Jafar that it's a big hassle because the stone is expensive and the carvings will have to be redone."

"Did they say why it fell?" Zet said.

"No. The obelisk was a four-sided needle shape, with a pointed top and carvings up and down its surface. Straight as an arrow, which is extremely hard to do. It would kill me if a piece of jewelry I'd spent months making was smashed like that."

"I wonder if someone sabotaged it?"

"That would be so evil," Hui said, blanching. "If it was close to the chapel, maybe they thought she'd walk out just as . . .?"

Zet pulled out the building plans. He handed the scroll through the bars.

Hui pored over it. "I see Senna marked the chapel for you." He moved his finger across the giant page, over the lines that represented walls, the breaks that symbolized door openings and the circles for pillars. He tapped a square shape. "This small square is the obelisk.

Look, Senna made a note beside it."

Zet eyed the scrawl. "That's a note?"

"I can't read too well, but I'm pretty sure that says *Obelisk*." He ran a finger back to the tiny chapel room. "They're pretty far apart. Too far."

NAUNET

After Zet and Hui had talked awhile longer, Zet said, "Who's the lady in the other cell?"

"I was wondering that, too. I asked the stable master. He told me to mind my own business."

Out of nowhere, something jolted Zet's memory. "I just figured out where I heard the sunburnt man's voice!"

"Where?"

"Talking to our boat Captain! The sunburnt man is the Captain's brother! Darius, that's his name." Zet quickly told him about the conversation he'd overheard.

"Sounds like they're not exactly close."

"I'd say. Still, they did go duck hunting together."

"And you said they have a sister here?" Hui said. "I wonder who she is?"

"Good question. But I just thought of something awful." He knocked his forehead against the bars. "Darius was on that duck hunting trip—he couldn't be the kidnapper."

From down the hall, the stable master bellowed, "Boy! What are you doin'?"

"*Beetle dung!*" Zet said.

"Can you come back later?" Hui said.

"I'll try!"

"Boy, didn't you hear me?" The stable master marched down the hall. "I thought you had a message to deliver, not a speech. This ain't no social club in here. You'll get me in trouble. Now go on, get out."

"Sorry, I'm going," Zet said.

Hui looked desperate as Zet said goodbye.

Zet felt equally so. Both of his leads had turned out false—the prints in the wadi led nowhere, and Darius had an alibi. He grabbed his head, his thoughts racing. He had to do something. But what?

"Why are you hanging 'round my door?" the stable master said, emerging from the barn. He looked like he was normally a nice guy, but really wanted to stay out of trouble.

"Sorry," Zet said, apologizing for the second time. "I wanted to ask you about these donkeys. Who uses them?"

"The workmen. Who do you think?"

"Was anyone using them the day the Priestess disappeared?"

"You ain't the first to wonder that. As it happens, one went missing all night. But it was back the following morning."

"Where was it?"

"Boy, donkeys can't speak. If we knew that, we knew where she'd got to, wouldn't we? Now I gotta get these donkeys in for the night."

"Thanks." Zet nodded and trudged off.

His feet carried him to the dinner tent. Lost in thought, he followed the line through the door. The crowd chattered and laughed, talking in loud voices about their day. He reached a long table from which the food was being served. A woman ladled vegetable stew into a clay bowl and handed it to Zet. Next, a second woman sliced a piece of meat from a roasted haunch and laid it on top of his stew. Further along, a deep basket held thick slices of warm bread. Zet grabbed two. The food smelled delicious, and his mouth watered.

He glanced around, looking for a place to sit.

The workmen sat in groups, filling the tent to capacity. He spotted Jafar and hesitated. If he sat there, he'd have to answer questions about Hui.

"Zet!" called a girl's voice.

He turned. He grinned when he spotted Naunet, and his heart raced a little. He was glad to see a friendly face, that's all. She had two other girls in tow, and was just leaving the food table.

"Hi," he said, approaching. "Can I sit with you?"

The two girls laughed, as if this were the funniest thing they'd ever heard.

Naunet, meanwhile, simply said, "We take our food back to the boat."

"Oh. Right. Of course."

"Come on," one of the girls said, frowning at her.

Naunet colored. "Hold on! I'm coming." Brushing her dark hair from her eyes she turned to Zet. "What happened to that boy?"

"He's going to have to stand trial."

"Well, he's definitely guilty. I couldn't believe it when I saw him with that bag! I almost fainted. Where is he? Where are they keeping him?"

"In a cell. By the way, do you know anything about a woman who's being held there?"

"A woman?" she said, her eyes widening.

"I saw a woman in a cell near his." Then, realizing she might wonder why he was visiting the prisoner, he added, "I had to check on the runner, so that I could make a report to my master."

She was watching his face, as if waiting for him to go on.

"And that's when I saw her. It was kind of creepy. Seeing a lady in there like that."

The other two girls with Naunet shifted nervously from foot to foot.

"You don't have to wait for me," she told them. "I'll catch up. I just want to talk to my friend for a minute."

The girls shot dubious looks at Zet, but they left.

"Sorry, we're supposed to keep to ourselves," she said.

"I don't want to get you in trouble."

"I think it's probably too late for that," she said with a small smile. "What I wanted to tell you is that we know her. The lady."

This staggered him. "You do? How, who is she?"

"She's a healer. Or was." Naunet paused. "She and her daughter helped care for the Priestess. The Priestess has some health issues."

Zet thought of what Senna told him. Again, he felt a shudder of unease roll through him at the thought of the Princess being sick and out somewhere locked up in the desert.

"The woman's daughter, Kissa, was with my mistress the day she disappeared. So was I."

"Wait, you *were there?*"

Naunet nodded. "Yes. Terrible isn't it?"

Zet wondered if she was going to start crying, so he stared into his dish of stew and waited for her to go on. "What happened?" he finally prompted, unable to contain his curiosity any longer. He couldn't believe he was about to get a first hand account.

"Everything was fine. It was a lovely day, and we were looking around in a little chapel that's being built near the edge of the site. But then we heard a loud crash. A great explosion, really. My mistress sent me to see what it was. I ran through the construction site. All the way to the courtyard. An obelisk had fallen. Pieces had flown everywhere. Clouds of dust filled the air, people were screaming and shouting."

He and Hui had been thinking the obelisk was meant to kill someone.

But wait—could it have been used as a distraction?

Naunet clutched her dinner bowl so tightly that her fingers were white. "I ran back to the chapel to tell her. She and Kissa were gone." Raising her chin, she looked Zet in the eye. "At first, I thought they left without me and headed back here. But they hadn't."

Her face was stoic. Zet wondered if she blamed herself. Or if others blamed her.

"Why did they lock Kissa's mother up?"

Naunet's face turned dark. "Kissa is a Hyksos!"

Zet's mouth dropped open.

"Yes," Naunet said, shaking. "She's a Hyksos, our sworn enemy. The very people our army has been fighting against to take back our lands! All this time they've been hiding the truth, but they were found out. They were spies. They were in on it!"

Zet's mind reeled. Why hadn't Senna told him this?

Naunet stared at the ground. Softly, she said, "You just never know who to trust, do you?"

"No," Zet murmured.

"I wish I could sit here and eat with you," she said suddenly. "I really do. I feel like I can talk to you. Even though we've barely met, I feel like you're the first friend I've had in a long time."

At this, Zet grinned. "I don't think the other girls would like that too much!"

She laughed. "That's for sure. There are a lot of rules. And everyone's always maneuvering for control. It's . . . competitive. You never know who's being nice and who's just trying to get something."

"Sounds awful," he said, feeling guilty for trying to pick her brains. He really did like her though. "Why don't you quit?"

Her eyes twinkled. "I just might. But I'd better get back to my boat. I'm probably in big trouble already."

"Maybe I should come and tell them to leave you alone?" Zet said, beaming.

"Probably not a good idea!" But she was laughing.

21

DISASTER

Outside the tent, Zet took a deep draught of stew. It was delicious. Hunger took over, and he shoveled more into his mouth with his bread. He was halfway finished, and wondering if they'd give him seconds if he went back inside, when he spotted Ari.

Senna's tall servant made a beeline for him.

"You're safe," Ari said, obviously relieved.

"Why wouldn't I be?" Zet asked.

"You need to come with me."

Zet wasn't leaving until he'd downed his dinner. He did so, and then darted inside to return the bowl. He looked longingly at the food. Men were lined up for seconds. Then Ari was at his elbow pulling him outside.

"Senna's boat was ransacked," Ari said in a low voice. "While Senna was away reporting to the medjay. They found the scroll you brought from Thebes."

"Uh oh."

"Your cover's not blown, yet. That scroll didn't mention you by name. The Queen Mother's spy could be any of the men who came on the boat with you."

"Yes, but I'm Senna's new runner. They'll suspect me first."

"That's why you're to sleep on Senna's boat tonight. It's safer. Medjay Commander's orders."

Zet spotted Senna's boat, bobbing against the wharf. "No. It will look too suspicious."

Ari raised one eyebrow. "You can't be thinking of sleeping in your tent."

"I'll take my chances."

"Talk to Senna. He's waiting for you."

When Zet entered Senna's cabin, he found the man looking flustered and irritated. Scrolls and shards of ostraca lay scattered across the room. It had been messy before, but now it was a disaster.

"Why didn't you tell me about the Hyksos woman?" Zet blurted.

Senna looked up, arms full, white brows jutting like bird feathers. "I forgot."

"You forgot? That's she's Hyksos? The enemy?"

"Since she's locked up, she's no threat now. Anyway, she denies it."

"Still, why didn't you tell me? I need to know these things!"

"And now you do," he snapped.

Fury rose in Zet and he forced it back down. No good would come of arguing with Senna. He pulled the building plans from his belt and handed them over.

"Thank you. Now unless you have anything useful to report, I need to get back to work." Not waiting for an answer, he turned away.

"I'll be sleeping in my tent," Zet told him.

"As you wish," Senna said in a sour tone.

THE TENT FELT INCREDIBLY empty without his best friend. He and Hui had set out on this together, thinking it would be an adventure. How had everything gone so wrong?

Zet's mind wandered back to Thebes. Home seemed so far away, like another world.

Kat would be sick with worry if she knew Hui was going to stand trial for stealing the royal jewels. As would Hui's mother Delilah, and his four younger brothers. With good reason. Hui would be killed for it. Unless Zet cleared his name.

Thank the gods they didn't know.

Zet's mind flew from one thing to the next. He'd forgotten to ask Hui what the priest wanted. Then he thought of the bag of jewels. Maybe Kissa's mother hid them in the river, tied to that branch? Before she got caught?

Around and around he went, thinking of the wadi and the arrest, the priest and Hui in his cell, the missing donkey, and the break-in at Senna's boat. He lay back, flopping one arm over his eyes. As he drifted off to sleep, his last thought was that he needed to hide the seal ring.

He woke with a start. It was pitch black.

Sweat broke out across his chest. Was someone outside?

He crept on all fours and pressed one eye to the door. The dark world was silent, apart from the gentle swish of water slapping against the harbor and the creak of boats.

Wide awake, he crawled through the flap.

Not a soul in sight.

When his stomach growled, he jumped at the noise. Then he almost laughed. The noise seemed to be the theme song of his life right now. According to the cook, he wasn't the only hungry person in camp. Zet thought of the cook's missing meat pie.

Wait—could that be a clue?

Was it possible the kidnappers were taking food to some hideout? Little bits here and there, but not enough to rouse suspicion?

Zet caught his breath.

They could be hiding out across the river. That's why Darius wanted the skiff! To ferry food across the canal! But there, his theory fell apart. Darius never got the skiff. His brother refused to lend it to him. And Darius had an alibi, anyway.

Still, he couldn't shake the idea that Darius was involved.

An idea began to form. That duck hunting trip—Darius had access to the rowboat. He probably snuck off with it after dark, when his brother was asleep.

He could have rowed up the canal to the wadi, where his accomplices were keeping the Princess waiting. Then they forced the Princess into the boat and ferried her away. Maybe there was a hut on the canal's opposite bank. Or a cave. A place where they were keeping her. And they were stealing food and bringing it out there.

Excitement snaked along Zet's spine.

Could that be it?

He started walking toward the outdoor kitchen area. When he reached the dark mess tent, not a single shadow moved. He crossed back behind, toward the kitchen area and kept going. A thick date palm, fringed by tall grass, made a good hiding spot. He melted into the shadows to wait.

His gaze drifted to the barn. The long, low stable loomed black as ink. Stars and a partial moon gave just enough light to see that the door was unmanned. He pictured Hui inside. It must be locked up tight.

Then, to Zet's surprise, the door slowly opened.

A boy emerged, dressed in a cloak that covered him from head to toe. *Osiris's beard! Hui was escaping!*

He had a donkey by a rope bridle, and was leading it out the door.

Zet was about to shout Hui's name. Something stopped him.

Where would Hui get that cloak from? And Hui was bigger than that. Zet saw that now. The boy was coming closer. Zet flattened himself against the tree as the boy glanced his way.

The donkey was loaded down with saddlebags. Clearly the boy rode often, because he leaped onto the donkey's back with practiced ease. Where was he going at this hour? The boy pulled the bridle and turned the animal around. He kicked the donkey's flanks, and the animal took off.

The food, this boy was taking food! That had to be it!

Heart in his mouth, Zet sprinted after him.

22

NIGHT TREK

Away from the barn, the world was gray-black. Lizards scuttled through the dry grasses. At least, he hoped they were lizards. He remembered the scorpion he'd seen the other day, and his toes cringed as he ran. His household god, Bastet, the ebony cat, was far from this dark place. Still he sent out a silent prayer, asking for her protection.

Zet was a fast runner. The donkey and its rider were faster.

Breathing hard, Zet pushed himself until his heart hammered in his chest.

There would be no catching them. That grew painfully obvious.

Zet was pretty sure they were headed for the wadi. Maybe the kidnappers stole a boat from someone else. If the boy on the donkey planned to meet the kidnappers, it would take awhile to transfer the goods. And the men might want a report from him, too.

Zet might just make it in time.

With fresh hope, he ran on.

He knew he must have bypassed the construction site by now. He'd been running for at least twenty minutes, trying to follow the angle the donkey had taken. Tall brush rose around him. The wadi had to be close.

He slowed and sniffed the air, hoping to catch the brackish scent of the river.

The air smelled of dirt and sunburnt leaves.

He was lost.

Bearing left, the undergrowth grew thicker and thicker. Turning backwards grew difficult. Thorny plants grabbed at his bare legs. Jabbed into the soles of his feet. For all he knew, he was going in circles. With a shout of frustration, he ripped at the branches and sprinted, thorns cutting into him, his jaw tight with agony.

Finally, he burst free.

Sitting down, he plucked barbs from his toes and heels.

Too much time had passed. He'd never catch them at the river now, even if he did know the way. This trek had been completely useless. There was no point in going on. He only hoped he could find his way home.

The moon had risen higher, just enough to cast a glow on the outline of the desert mountains. Using them as a guide, he began to walk, keeping them to his left. After a long time, the pyramid came into view, jutting up to touch the stars.

He breathed out a sigh of relief.

By the time he reached the harbor, he was dragging his injured feet in exhaustion. He approached his tent. Even in his tired state, he knew it looked more crooked than how he'd left it. A sixth sense made the hairs on his forearms stand straight.

He swerved before he reached it, and softly padded for Senna's boat.

A medjay dozed at the end of the gangplank. The man came to with a start.

"Oh, it's just you," the medjay said, recognizing Zet. "Go on up."

On the forward deck, Senna had an outdoor sitting area. Cushions lay under a broad sunroof made of thick fabric. The feathered pillows fluffed up around him as he sank deeply into the luxurious mass. An instant later, he was fast asleep.

The following morning before dawn, footsteps woke him. Someone was running onto the ship.

A moment later, Senna could be heard grumbling. "By the snout of Anubis, what's the emergency?"

Ari murmured a reply that Zet couldn't quite catch.

Zet propped himself up on one elbow and rubbed his face.

What was going on?

He got to his feet and headed for the door to Senna's cabin. When he reached it, a boy not much older than Zet came out. He shot Zet an apologetic look. The next moment, Zet knew why. Senna was making angry noises, slamming things around.

"Zet!" Senna shouted.

Gulping, Zet went in.

"What happened?" Zet asked.

"This!" Senna held up a scroll in his fist and shook it. "This message is what happened!"

As the architect turned it over, the huge seal became visible. Anyone would recognize the marking stamped in thick wax. Pharaoh had written to Senna in the night.

Senna nodded, seeing Zet's face. "Yes, the Mighty Bull himself." Then he wrung the paper between his hands with a look of despair. "He's coming tomorrow morning!"

"Tomorrow! But . . . he wasn't supposed to be here for three more days!"

"Pharaoh does what he wants. And if that's arriving early, he'll do so."

"We have no idea where she is. That's not enough time." Zet's skin prickled with cold sweat.

"It will have to be. We've kept the secret from Pharaoh this long. But there will be no keeping it from him when he arrives."

"Wait, he doesn't know? How can he not know?"

Senna grimaced. "Queen Mother's orders."

"Can she do that? He'll be furious!"

"I never should have listened to her! He'll have to be told. He'll say it's my fault!" Senna swallowed, looking pale. "It'll be my neck. I might be Pharaoh's favorite architect, but Princess Merit is his favorite daughter. And then there are the Hyksos demands. He won't like it. He won't like it at all!" Senna sank down into a heavy slump and put his face in his hands. "He's coming early, because they've won a great battle. Imagine what he's going to say when he gets here and learns . . ."

"That the Hyksos want the barricade removed," Zet murmured.

"Yes. If Pharaoh does this, everything he's won will be lost. The Hyksos will continue south. Soon, they'll be fighting in Thebes."

The image of battle in Zet's hometown struck such fear into him that he felt sick. His wonderful town, with his family and their house, and their bright, happy stall in the market, it would all be destroyed.

What would Pharaoh do? Give up his daughter for the peace of Egypt? Let the Hyksos kill her so the rest of Egypt's people could live? Or save her and fight a losing battle? It was a horrible choice to face.

Zet had to do something, fast. Time had almost run out.

"I need to talk to Merimose," Zet said.

"Do what you will. I fear it will make little difference."

Outside, the deck was still cool and damp with dew. He pounded down the gangway and sprinted along the shore. Moments later, he reached the medjays' sturdy vessel. A broad-shouldered man stood on the watersteps, barring his entrance.

"I need to talk to Commander Merimose," Zet said, breathless.

"He's not—" he paused. "Hold on, I know you!"

In that instant Zet, recognized him, too. "You're the desk officer from the main office at Thebes!"

"And you're the pottery boy who won that big reward some months back," the man said with a grin. "But you can't talk to the Commander. He's not here."

23

THE LADY PRISONER

Zet should have figured Merimose wouldn't be there. He had to find him, fast. Before he could speak, the medjay leaned forward.

"Good news, though." The man's eyes flickered. "I think they found our missing Priestess."

Was it possible? "Where?"

"Can't say. But they'll be back in a few hours."

Zet let the news sink in. Was it possible they'd really found her? It was too much to be believed. Too much to hope for.

Cautiously, he said, "That's great."

"I'll relax when they get back," the medjay said, as if reading Zet's mind.

Zet knew he should report the news to Senna. Instead, he headed for the barn. He wanted to tell Hui first.

What had Merimose learned last night that had tipped the medjay off? He pondered this as he walked. And would finding the kidnappers get Hui off the hook? That wasn't guaranteed.

When he neared the pasture, a pair of floppy-eared donkeys milled about. One was gray, the other brown. They both had wide eyes, rimmed with thick lashes. As Zet passed, the brown one trotted over and stuck his nose over the bamboo enclosure.

"Hello," Zet said, laughing. He stroked the animal's soft nose. The other donkey approached, looking hopeful. "Sorry, I don't have a snack for you guys. Maybe next time."

Turning away, he made for the barn door. It was deserted. The stable master was probably still at breakfast. Zet pushed at the door and found it unlocked. He stepped inside, into the dusty gloom. Straw crunched as he walked, perfuming the still air.

Movement caught his attention.

He glanced left, through the bamboo bars. It was the cell with the Hyksos woman. She sat against the far wall, looking wide-awake and cautious.

Their eyes met.

Zet's first thought was that she didn't look Hyksos. She looked like any normal Egyptian. Dark hair and intelligent, almond shaped eyes.

"Good morning," the woman said, with no trace of foreign accent.

"Hello," Zet replied. He was tempted to question her, but kept walking.

"Wait," the woman called after him. She rose and hurried to the bars. Worried lines creased her forehead. "Has there been any news?"

"Of the Priestess?" Zet said.

"Yes, and the girl who was with her."

"Your daughter?"

Her proud shoulders sagged. "Ah. So you know."

"I do." He studied her face. "I never would have guessed you're Hyksos. I'm not surprised people were fooled."

"I am not Hyksos. Whoever told you that is a liar. But I suppose the whole camp believes it now."

Zet frowned. "There's no point in keeping up your story. The medjay know."

"That's where you're wrong. They know the truth. I told them I could prove it, and begged them not to smear my name. They gave me their word. I guess their word means nothing!"

Zet was completely confused. "Well, if you're not Hyksos, what are you?"

"I'm Egyptian!" she cried. Her cheeks had turned a deep shade of red. With apparent effort, she seemed to calm herself. "I'm Egyptian," she repeated quietly.

"And your daughter?"

"We're innocent!" she said, and then clammed up.

"My friend is being held in another cell. He's tied up in all of this. They think he stole something, and he might have to stand trial. If you've already told the medjay, and if you're innocent like you say, what's the harm in telling me the truth? If you're not Hyksos spies, and you didn't hatch this kidnapping plot, surely you'd want to help me?"

The woman was silent for a long time.

Zet was growing antsy. He thought she was going to refuse, to send him on his way. He was about to leave when she nodded.

"All right," she said. "I grew up in a village in the North of Egypt. Next to the Hyksos border. In my fifteenth year, Hyksos warriors invaded our village. I was kidnapped, taken from everyone and everything I loved."

Zet watched her face. Her cheeks were flushed and her breathing had increased. She looked frightened, as if she were living it all over again.

She let go of the bars and wiped her hands on her linen skirt. "Still, I survived. Things could have been worse. I'd been learning the healing arts. I saved a dying man, and that earned me a little respect with my captors. But when a Hyksos warrior took me as his bride, I was desperate to escape. I tried and failed many times. Things grew worse when we had a daughter. Seeing her tiny face, I knew I had to get away or die." Her face was hard. "I refused to let her be raised as Hyksos, sworn enemies of my people!"

"What did you do?"

"I didn't run, like the other times. I secretly sold one of my husband's jeweled daggers and bartered for passage south. Traders smuggled me and my daughter aboard a trading vessel, hidden in rolls of carpets! We went all the way to Thebes, as far as we could get."

The story was too fantastic to be a lie. He suspected she spoke the truth.

"How did you go from being runaways to working with—"

He almost said Princess Meritamon. But it was too late. Her eyes widened. She knew.

Out loud, she said, "The Priestess was born with an illness. Her back is curved, and it affects her terribly. Meanwhile, my reputation as a healer was growing." She smiled sadly. "Her father heard about me, and the rest is history. My daughter and I went to live in her household. Kissa was learning my skills. But she's not just a healer, they're close friends."

"So you never told them your daughter is part Hyksos?"

Her cheeks colored. "No. Not even Kissa knows."

Zet's jaw dropped.

"She was a baby!" the woman said. "She didn't choose her father. She's loyal and honest and wouldn't hurt a mosquito."

"Then why did you tell the medjay about her now?"

"I didn't. Two men from my old village did. They saw me and recognized me, and remembered," she said with a miserable laugh. "Manu and Darius."

"Darius," Zet repeated.

She drew away. "You know him?"

"A tall, sunburnt man with a round belly? We're not friends. He attacked me at the construction site."

Zet's thoughts were racing. Darius grew up on the border with the Hyksos. Understanding fell into place. Darius would do anything for quick profit. Even his own brother, the boat Captain, said so. Had Darius approached the Hyksos, or had they approached him? How much were they paying him to be their spy? How many other evil acts had Darius committed for the enemy against his own people?

Did Merimose and the other medjay know Darius was guilty?

Zet wanted to ask more questions, but the entrance creaked open.

A shaft of light illuminated the straw dust that floated in the warm air.

The stable master entered, carrying what appeared to be breakfast. He paused at the sight of Zet, and his brow furrowed in a dark line.

"What are you doing in here?" he demanded.

"I came to talk to the runner."

"My fault," the woman added. " I stopped him to see if there's news. Is there?"

"No," the man growled. "And the runner's not here. You need to leave. Now."

"The runner's not here? Where is he?" Zet said.

"That priest came for him this morning. That's all I know."

24

GLIMMERS OF FEAR

When Zet stumbled back out into the sunlight, he stared across the paddock in confusion.

Why had the Priest of Osiris taken Hui away?

And on whose authority?

Maybe Senna would know. He headed for the architect's boat. Then he realized he'd better hurry. He hadn't reported in with the news that Merimose had a lead on the Princess. Senna would still be worried out of his mind.

As he ran however, he couldn't help pondering what he'd learned from the woman. Darius had gone to the medjay about her. If the medjay trusted him, they were wrong. Was it possible Darius would do something to stop the men? What if he'd set a trap?

The hopeful feeling he'd felt earlier started to fade.

A small voice inside warned him something was off. He wished he could talk to Merimose. But he had no way of learning where the medjay had gone.

A calm had fallen over the waterfront. Far overhead, tiny birds circled in the vast blue sky. In the bay, several fish broke the surface, flashing into the air. They skimmed across the water, appearing and disappearing. A bird swooped down and snapped one up in its beak. The harbor surface turned dead calm.

SENNA HADN'T YET HEARD the news. The wrinkled old architect listened to Zet with eyes that were more wary than hopeful.

"Do you know what the priest wanted with Hui?" Zet asked.

"No idea." He shoved a basket of ostraca Zet's way.

"What are these?" Zet said, staring down at the white, pottery shards covered in Senna's scribbled hieratic.

"Messages for my workers. Now that you're no longer the Queen Mother's spy, it's time you got to work."

"But they haven't actually found her—"

"That's no longer your concern. The temple construction will go on! And until you're excused from duty, you work for me."

"But I could still—"

"This one here is for Hori," Senna said, picking out a shard. "You'll know him by his red belt." He went on and on. There were so many shards, Zet had no idea how he'd keep them straight.

"Put the strap over your head," Senna advised, "There you go. Excellent."

With the leather shoulder strap slung across his chest, Zet had to lean sideways not to fall over. He couldn't believe he was going to do this, when the case wasn't yet solved! Then again, at least he'd be out running around. He'd run out of leads. Sure, he could ignore Senna's orders and take off, but with what purpose?

He set out to find Hori.

It turned out Hori had a message to take back to Senna. To Zet's dismay, so did everyone who received one of Zet's shards. Even worse, most he just had to memorize, because few of the men bothered to write them down. And every single person he asked about the missing priestess stared at him blankly.

"I don't know nothing about that!" said one.

"Don't involve me, I got my job to think about," said another.

By the time he'd made his fourth trip, he climbed on board Senna's boat, he was sweaty, frustrated and bordering on furious. "Wouldn't it be easier to go there and set up camp for the day?"

"Do you realize how hot it is outside?" Senna cried, raising his fluffy brows.

Zet mopped sweat from his face and arms. Senna handed him another basket.

"Now hurry!" Senna said. "These are important. They've put the wrong foundation stones down. The wall is liable to fall over."

And so Zet dashed out into the blazing heat.

Lunch came and still the medjay hadn't returned. The fissure of worry he'd felt that morning was growing. He'd managed to detour by the barn and learn from the annoyed stable master that *'no, Hui was not back yet'*.

Somehow he managed to choke down some food, but his stomach felt jittery.

By late afternoon, patches of ground that had burned his feet earlier grew dark with shadow. An unusual coolness settled over the valley. His sweat turned chill. Zet shivered.

Back on the waterfront, he glanced toward the medjay's boat. The same man who'd been there in the morning still stood at the foot of the gangplank.

Otherwise, it was deserted.

Ra, the sun god, hovered on the horizon.

What could have happened? What could be taking them so long?

Was it possible the medjay had been led into a trap? Or on a wild goose chase?

When dinner came and went, Zet's stomach began to cramp with fear. Something had definitely gone wrong.

Merimose and his men could be in real trouble right now. Hyksos could have ambushed them. Maybe Merimose was somewhere in the desert, fighting for his life.

And what of Hui?

Zet swallowed down a horrible dizzy feeling.

It was his fault Hui had come here. If something happened to Hui, the guilt and horror of losing his best friend would kill him.

Workers were filing toward the dinner tent, laughing and talking like everything was normal. For them, it was. Zet couldn't even think about eating. When he spotted Jafar, Zet turned away and slunk into the shadows. He ran straight into Naunet.

She smiled, but her smile quickly faded. "Are you all right?"

Suddenly, he wanted to tell her everything. He needed to talk to someone, and he felt sure she'd understand. Then he remembered—she thought Hui was a thief.

He nodded. "Yes, everything's okay."

"I wanted to ask if you want to bring your dinner and eat at the watersteps by our boat?" she said, coloring.

"Really?" To his dismay, he felt his own face growing hot. What was the matter with him? Anyway, he couldn't. He had to find Hui. Right now. "Thanks, I really want to. But I can't."

"Another time," she said, sounding disappointed.

Running on silent feet, he ran for the barn. When it came into view, he slowed. The stable master stood chatting with a few workers out front. Zet skirted through the tall grass, making his way around back.

He went to the end of the building, feeling pretty sure he'd reached Hui's cell wall. Then he picked up a loose stone and tapped it against the mud bricks.

"Come on, Hui," he whispered. *"Be in there!"*

Crickets hummed. Distant chatter and the smell of roast game wafted on the breeze.

Zet knocked again, harder this time.

"Hui! It's me!" he whispered.

There was a short pause. Then, a soft chink of metal against stone rang out from the opposite side of the wall.

Zet's breath caught.

Hui was there!

The tapping came again, several hand-widths away from where Zet stood. Zet moved toward the sound. He knew Hui had been digging the mortar from between the stones in his cell. This must be the place. He tapped the rock to be sure, and an excited tapping came from the other side.

Zet found a sharper stone. He started digging at the sun-dried mud that sealed the bricks together. Hui was clearly doing the same. Together they worked hard and fast. Zet was terrified they'd be caught. Still, he kept working.

No way was he letting Hui stay in there any longer.

Suddenly, the tip of a blade shot through to Zet's side. It glimmered in the moonlight, and disappeared back between the bricks.

"I'm through, aren't I!" Hui whispered.

"Yes! Don't stop," Zet whispered back.

Soon Hui's blade appeared more easily, stabbing out in various spots along the wall.

"Start kicking," Hui said.

"Stand back," Zet whispered.

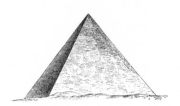

25

RUN!

*Z*et glanced both ways. Then he delivered a hard kick to the wall. The bricks held firm.

"Come on!" He slammed into it with a second kick. His bare foot stung with the force of the blow. He kicked it a third time. The wall shook a little, but didn't break.

"Harder!" Hui whispered.

Zet backed twenty steps away. He sprinted forward and launched a kick so powerful that the force of his strike sent him flying onto his behind.

The bricks shuddered. And cracked inward. Hui's hands appeared, and then his face. He grinned at Zet through the hole.

"Lying down on the job, I see," he whispered.

"Ow?" Zet said, half laughing, half groaning as he rubbed his foot.

Hui broke his way through and stretched his arms. "Freedom!"

"Not yet," Zet said, "But I'm pretty sure Darius stole those jewels. And I think he's sent the medjay into an ambush. And come to think of it, I haven't seen him all day."

They talked quickly. Zet told him about the donkey with the food supplies, and how he felt sure it had gone to the canal last night.

"Their camp must be on the opposite bank," Zet said.

"Do you think the rider will bring food there again tonight?"

"Possibly. Food and messages. I suspect the kidnappers are still over there with her, and whatever trap the medjay have fallen into is as far as you can get from that place. On this side of the water, in the mountains or something."

"We could wait here," Hui said. "Until the rider comes for a donkey. But that might be dangerous."

"Agreed. What if we go to the wadi and hide out? And if the boy doesn't come, we'll find a way across the canal before dawn and start searching."

"How wide is it?" Hui said.

In the big ferry, it had seemed narrow. But standing on the bank had been a different story. "You don't want to know."

They crept around the far end of the barn and paused. The stable master still stood talking with his friends near the door. Despite the darkness, he and Hui would have to move carefully not to be seen.

In the far distance stood the hulking mountains. The Traveler—the moon god Khonsu—rested between the peaks. Soon Khonsu would forge his way through the shimmering stars.

"We'll have to go around the paddock," Zet whispered. "Make a run for it on the far side."

Hui nodded.

Ducking low, they skirted along the enclosure. A furry cluster of donkeys nosed at the ground, looking for grass. Zet and Hui reached the far side, when Zet noticed gate access into the donkey pen.

On impulse, he tried the handle. It lifted easily.

"Come on," he whispered, opening it and squeezing through.

"I'm liking this idea," Hui whispered.

"Why walk when you can ride?" Zet said, pulse racing.

He spotted the brown donkey he'd seen earlier that day. "Hey, Brownie," he said, taking hold of its rope. To his relief, the soft-nosed creature followed him out the gate. Zet scrambled up onto its back.

Meanwhile, Hui was still dodging amongst the pack. He yelped, barely missing a kick from a big donkey. Another almost took a chomp of his fingers.

"Quit playing around. Let's go!" Zet hissed.

"What do you think I'm doing?"

Zet was growing more nervous. "The stable master's going to bring them inside any minute. Hurry up!"

"Tell that to my gray-eared friend here!" Hui said, waving a handful of grass under a small donkey's nose. The donkey took the bait and trotted after him. Hui shut the gate and clambered on top.

Zet gave his animal a nudge. "Come on Brownie. Let's get away from here."

Brownie started into a happy trot. But when Zet looked back, he saw Hui's animal hadn't budged. Shouts came from the barn. *Flea dung!*

"A little help?" Hui said.

Zet trotted back to Hui. "Toss me your rope!"

Hui did. "Wake up, Gray Ears! It's adventure time!"

After Zet gave Gray Ears' rope a few tugs, it reluctantly started forward. And then they were off. Zet headed for the construction site. He didn't want to risk getting lost like the night before. He kept turning back to peer into the darkness, sure he'd see the stable master coming after them.

Soon, it became clear they'd gotten away.

Zet shot a grin at Hui. His best friend's wide grin shone back at him in the moonlight. It felt great to be back on the chase together!

Hui whooped. Zet did the same.

Riding made everything go so much faster. He hadn't spent much time on a donkey, his animal was tame and required little direction. Hui's seemed happy to follow, as long as Zet had hold of the rope. They reached the chapel in no time. From there, Zet was able to find the wadi without too much trouble. Being higher up on the donkey's back had advantages. He could see farther.

They reached the broad, ink-black canal and stopped.

The surface flowed quickly, making sucking, gurgling sounds where it rushed against the shore.

"*Sobek's fangs*, I hope we don't have to swim across that," Hui said.

They sat for a long moment, staring.

"The boy will come," Zet said, trying to convince himself as much as Hui.

"You're not going to like this, but—maybe the rider's just a boy stealing food for his family."

They looked at one another. Zet pondered this horrible possibility.

"We better find someplace to hide," Hui said.

A stand of rushes far down the bank provided the only spot. But there was nowhere to tie the animals. Hui, master of all things trickster-like, came up with the idea to tie each animal's lead rope around its two front legs. They could move, but couldn't take off.

"Not that Gray Ears will run anywhere," Hui said with a grin, patting his donkey.

Then they hurried back to the river to wait.

And wait . . .

Khonsu, the moon god, reached his zenith in the sky, and still no one had come. The chill air was making Zet stiff. He wanted to get up and stretch. And he was getting worried.

Suddenly, he heard something.

"Someone's coming," he whispered and ducked lower.

26

THE BOY AND HIS DONKEY

The small boy approached, riding quickly.

Zet wanted to jump up and tackle him. Good sense won out.

The boy's hood hid his face. Still, it was clear he didn't expect to be followed. He didn't even bother to look around. He simply led his donkey to the water's edge.

Zet frowned. There was no boat in sight.

Then the boy did something strange. He tucked the long sides of his cloak up underneath himself until he was sitting on them. Then he settled back in place.

With a kick of his pale heels, he urged the animal forward down the riverbank. Soon water rushed over the donkey's front hooves. Again, the boy kicked the beast. He made a clicking noise with his tongue, urging the donkey on. Finally it gave in.

In amazement, Zet watched it wade up to its flanks.

And then the donkey began moving across the wide canal.

Swimming.

The donkey was swimming. That's how they got across. No wonder Darius wanted that skiff! It would be a lot better than this.

"Come on," Zet said.

Hui was already on his feet.

They ran for their animals. Getting them into the canal was another matter. Zet and Hui pushed and pulled. Finally they managed to do it. Despite the struggle, the donkeys were strong swimmers. But the delay had lost precious time.

The boy was just a small figure in the darkness when Zet and Hui reached the far side. The donkeys waded out and shook, sending water in all directions.

"Good boy, Brownie," Zet cried. "Now hurry, before we lose him!"

The partial moon rose steadily higher, but the foliage was thick.

The boy vanished in the tall, weaving grasses. They spotted him again, far up ahead. Together, they followed the boy for close to an hour. Zet thanked the gods they had the donkeys. Brownie plodded steadily onward. Zet patted its neck in gratitude.

In the distance, the boy never bothered to turn around. Again, Zet wondered if the boy was simply a thief stealing food for his family.

A dark mass of trees blotted out the starry sky. They passed into the grove. Thick trunks broke the scrubby undergrowth. Date palms swayed overhead. The palm leaves made shush-shush sounds in the gentle wind. The air smelled sweet. Clusters of heavy fruit hung from reedy stalks.

Soon, the flowery scent mixed with the smell of brackish water.

He heard a rushing river. The Nile. After they left the canal, they must have cut across land at an angle to meet up with it.

A faint light glowed ahead. Then he saw a mud brick building. It looked like some kind of old storage facility. Maybe shippers used it to store goods on their way up and down the river. Whatever the case, the cloaked boy headed straight for it.

"Stop," Zet whispered.

Hui nodded his chin at the date palms. "We can tie up back there."

They did so, and then snuck as close to the building as they dared.

It was smaller than Zet first thought. Just a shack. Down on their bellies, they crawled around the perimeter. A poorly constructed lean-to came into view. It was set up to guard the front door. Zet spotted sleeping pallets under the makeshift shelter. Lamplight flickered. The air was smoky.

They crawled further and spotted a smoldering fire. Three men stood around it, talking to the boy. Someone laughed.

The boy's donkey was tethered next to two others.

One man went to unload the saddlebags and Zet saw his face. *Darius.*

"I hope you brought something good!" Darius said. "This calls for a celebration."

"We'll be rich," said the man who still wore his leather wrist-guards over his thick forearms. Manu, the other traitor from the border village.

"That we will," Darius agreed. "The medjay are dead, so we're in the clear. I guarantee they weren't expecting to meet a band of Hyksos in the mountains."

Zet listened to the news in horror. Merimose, dead? He wouldn't think about it now, he couldn't.

While Darius unloaded the supplies, the third man stoked the fire.

Since the kidnappers only had three donkeys tied up—the boy's and two others—Zet guessed the third man stayed all day to guard the prisoners. Then Darius and Manu came here straight from the worksite, after spending the day keeping their eyes on Senna and the medjay for signs of trouble. As for the boy, they had him pack up food when people went to sleep and steal out here to feed them.

At the thought of the prisoners, Zet's heart began to slam. Princess Meritamon was inside that shack! Just yards away.

The man by the fire emptied the contents of one sack into a cook pot. Then he stuck the cook pot right into the smoking coals.

"Three men," Hui whispered, his mouth close to Zet's head. "And we don't have weapons."

Zet stared grimly at the little group. He motioned Hui backwards.

"We have to get them away from there," he whispered.

Hui nodded, mischief beginning to flicker in his eyes. "Distraction time."

They snuck back to the date grove and worked out a plan.

"Poor chumps," Hui said. "They're in for a surprise."

It was easy to joke around, but they both knew the danger they were in. If things went wrong, this would turn deadly. Smart or not, Zet and Hui were just boys. If it came to a fight, they'd never win against full-grown men. They'd be killed, and no one would ever know what had happened to them.

In the dark, Zet and Hui did their old secret handshake for good luck. Then Hui darted away. Zet headed back for the shack. He lay on his belly in the dark. Insects crawled over him, tickling any bare flesh they could find. Finally, from far in the distance came the sound of splashing.

Hui had reached the Nile.

At the hut, all heads turned.

"What was that?" muttered Manu.

A soft, higher voice spoke. The boy. "Someone's coming from the river!"

"Shut up and let me listen," Darius snapped.

The splashing came again. Then a voice boomed, "Who's over there? At my shack?"

A second voice said, "Wait, it might be thieves!"

Hui sounded so convincing, even Zet was almost fooled.

Darius leaped to his feet. He grabbed his knife and stuffed it in his waistband. The others did the same. They squinted in the direction of the Nile. It was impossible to see. A papyrus forest, twice as high as any man, stood along its edge.

From the papyrus's depths, the deep voice spoke again. It was a forced whisper, but one designed to carry.

"Into the boat," the voice said. "We'll head back and get the others."

The splashing came again.

When Zet saw the way Darius bared his teeth in a grin, Zet felt sick. The yellow stumps shone in the moonlight.

Darius waved the other two men forward. "Quietly," he said. Then, to the boy, "Stay and keep an eye out."

At this Zet scowled. Just what he needed. If Zet tackled him, the boy could shout a warning.

The boy moved closer to the shack's barricaded door. As for the three men, they left the circle of light and made for the river.

And for Hui.

27

THE SHACK

The underbrush swallowed the three men to their chests. It would take another few minutes to reach the tall papyrus. When they got there, Hui would lead them further up river. Still, Zet had to act fast.

The boy stared off, watching the thugs.

Silently, Zet approached. At the last moment, the boy must have sensed him because he began to whirl. Zet grabbed him from behind and clamped his hand over the boy's mouth. The boy stiffened in shock. Then he began to struggle. He was smaller than Zet but wiry.

"Shut up or you're dead," Zet hissed, panicked they'd be heard.

The boy kept struggling. His hood fell over his face, almost to his chin. He wrenched forward and managed a muffled cry before Zet's hand clamped back in place.

Zet's heart pounded in terror. "I swear I'll kill you!"

He'd never do such a thing, but he hoped he sounded convincing. To his relief, the boy stopped struggling and went limp.

A shout from the Nile sent tremors of fear shooting through him.

"Pull out your swords, men!" shouted a deep voice. Hui's.

What was he doing? He was going to get himself killed!

Sweating in fear, Zet kept hold of him. He had to free the prisoners.

Now. He forced the kid around to face the door to the hut. A long wooden bar blocked it from the outside. The boy tried to bite Zet's palm, but Zet had been expecting something like that. He squeezed the boy's cheeks on either side with his thumb and forefinger.

The wild kid bit down on empty air. Then he started struggling again.

With one arm around the boy's neck and the other over his mouth, Zet kicked at the wooden bar. It rose slightly from its housing, but not enough to open the door. He kicked again, a second and a third time. With every kick, he felt sure the men would hear. The fourth time, the bar came up and over the wooden support that held it in place.

The door eased outward a fraction.

Zet drove his adversary up against the wall beside it and wrenched the door open with one hand. The boy nearly got away, but Zet quickly grabbed him and pushed him forward. Together, they tumbled into the little room.

Inside, the boy stood panting like a wild animal.

Zet didn't dare let go. He reached back and yanked the door shut.

A lamp burned on the floor. Two grimy girls sat against the wall, watching. They were on a sleeping pallet. The girls were wide-eyed. One looked terrified. The other uncertain but hopeful.

Despite their grime, and the fact that Zet had never seen her up close, he immediately recognized the second one as Princess Meritamon. She wasn't smiling like the girl at the royal festivals, but neither did she cower in fear. Her eyes, shaped like almonds, curved up slightly at the corners. She gave Zet a fast, frank assessment, with a confidence that could only come from being the daughter of Pharaoh himself.

"What's going on?" she demanded.

"Help me," Zet said, still holding the struggling boy. "Find something to tie him up!"

The other girl—Kissa—shrank against the wall.

"Him?" Princess Meritamon said. "Gladly. But that's no boy."

"What are you talking about?" Zet said.

"See for yourself."

Zet grabbed at the boy's hood, and his struggles increased. When he yanked the rough cloth down, a mass of hair tumbled free. Familiar eyes flashed as they met his. Zet felt like he'd been punched in the stomach.

"Naunet?" he said.

She gazed at him. "Why did you have to get in the middle of this, Zet?" Her voice was soft but heart-wrenching.

He stared at her in confusion. This had to be a mistake!

Tears appeared at the corner of her eyes.

Then she opened her mouth to scream. Shocked and devastated, he covered her mouth just in time.

Naunet's warning scream turned into a muffled cry.

Meanwhile, Kissa and Princess Meritamon ripped the sheet that covered their sleeping palette into several strips. As the Princess moved, Zet suddenly saw how curved her back was. It looked painful, and the thought of her trapped like this made him sick.

How could Naunet have done this? Zet had believed she was his friend. He'd trusted her.

"Tie her up," the Princess told Kissa. "Hurry."

Naunet kicked and bit, but Zet managed to tie a strip around her face. He felt horrible.

Once they'd tied Naunet's hands and feet, they lay her on the sleeping palette. Zet opened the door. The coast was clear.

"Come on," Zet said.

Princess Meritamon said, "Why should I trust you?"

"Why? I just helped tie up one of your kidnappers! Now come on!"

"You tied her up, yes. But you're certainly not a medjay. Or a palace guard. *She* seemed to know you well enough. Who are you working for?"

"You think I risked my life against those men because I'm a kidnapper, too?"

Kissa looked panicked. "Highness, we'd better go!"

"Not until he tells me why we should trust him. I have no intention of trading one group of kidnappers for another."

The men would be back any moment. Zet hadn't planned on this. He felt ill! If they didn't hurry . . . Then he remembered something—all those times he'd been warned to bury the coronation ring, and he hadn't. He reached into his tunic and pulled it out. He thrust it before her eyes.

"Grandmother's ring!" she gasped.

"She gave it to me, and sent me to find you."

Her eyes narrowed. "Tell me your name."

"Zet."

At this she nodded. "Help me up. She told me about you. Let's get out of here."

Outside, the fire still smoldered, casting off a wide pool of light. The three of them stepped through the door. He bolted it shut on Naunet. One arm circling the Princess's waist, he led her toward the darkness. Then he heard a shout across the broad expanse of scrubby fields.

"Faster, they're coming," the Princess said.

"I don't want to hurt you," he replied.

"Better hurt than dead," she gasped.

He broke into a run and dragged her with him. "Our donkeys are tied to the date trees," he shouted to Kissa. "Run and untie them!"

Kissa came to life, sprinting into the gloom. Zet glanced back. He should have untied the kidnappers' donkeys. He could have scattered them! Too late now.

Where was Hui?

From behind, the kidnappers' shouts grew louder.

28

ANSWERS IN THE NIGHT

Zet's breath was growing ragged. Still he kept running, half-carrying Princess Meritamon with him.

He heard Manu shout, "They're headed for the trees!"

"Stop them!" shouted Darius.

The men were gaining.

Then, from up ahead, their two donkeys burst from the grove. Hui was leading Brownie at a run, and Kissa was riding Gray Ears. Thank the gods! Zet tightened his hold around Princess Meritamon's waist, lifting her almost off the ground, and sprinted.

"Get them!" Darius roared, enraged. He sounded just yards away.

Hui threw Brownie's bridle rope toward Zet.

Zet caught it. Taking hold of the Princess with both hands, he lifted her with a strength he didn't know he had. She landed astride the donkey. Zet leaped up in front of her.

Darius was only three strides away.

The princess screamed as Darius latched onto her leg. Zet crooked his elbow, and putting all of his weight into it, slammed it in Darius's face. Darius fell back just long enough for Zet to kick his donkey into action. Brownie, clearly spooked, took off like a shot toward Hui.

Manu had reached them now, too. The huge man lunged at Hui and Kissa, but Gray Ears skittered sideways.

Zet scooped up Gray Ears' bridle rope. And then they were charging together through the date grove. Princess Meritamon tightened her arms around his waist. With sudden clarity, he realized just how amazing this was. He was riding on a donkey with a princess clinging to him.

But they weren't out of danger yet.

The men were doubling back for their own mounts. Zet angled left.

"Stick to the trees for as long as we can," Zet called back to Hui.

Hui nodded. He and Kissa were bent forward, giving Gray Ears its head.

The group stayed within the grove's cover until finally they were forced into the open. But it wasn't exactly open. Thorny branches tore at their legs. Zet's donkey slowed. Painfully, they picked their way forward.

Soon, overgrown bushes closed behind them.

"I think we lost them," Zet said softly.

"Agreed," Hui said in a low voice. "But we still have to cross the canal."

Zet glanced back at the Princess. "Are you all right?"

She nodded, but her cheeks were pinched and her eyes looked dark with pain.

Kissa spoke up. "I have my satchel. I can mix some herbs. It would only take . . ."

"No," Princess Meritamon said. Then in a parched sounding voice she added, "I'm fine. Unless someone has water?"

Zet wished he could help her. "Sorry. We didn't bring any."

She nodded. "But you came and got us. That's more than enough."

The journey was far from over, he thought. *And the danger.* To distract himself from his worry, he let his thoughts wander to Naunet. Her betrayal had left a painful spot in the middle of his chest. He guessed it would be there for a long time.

As he rode and thought of her, another piece of the mystery fell together. He recalled that conversation he'd overheard between Darius and the boat Captain.

"I hope you're not leaving without saying hello to Nan," Darius had said.

"If I see her tonight, good," the Captain had replied. *"If not, give my little sister my regards".*

Nan was a nickname. They'd been talking about Naunet. Darius, the Captain and Naunet were siblings. It seemed obvious now. How could he have missed it? How could he have trusted her?

With heavy heart, he imagined Naunet and Darius plotting the kidnapping.

He knew exactly how they'd done it.

First, Darius went upriver with the Captain on a 'hunting trip'.

Then, Manu and the other man weakened the obelisk by chiseling at the base during the night. The next morning, Naunet convinced the Princess to visit the chapel. When the obelisk crashed, Naunet ran to 'investigate'. In truth, she went to inform Manu that the Princess was alone in the chapel as planned.

While everyone was distracted, Manu moved in and snatched the Princess and Kissa. Naunet rushed back to the harbor, screaming that the Priestess had disappeared—but only after she'd given the men plenty of time to escape.

Darius was upriver. He snuck off with the skiff and rowed to the wadi. There he ferried the two girls across the canal.

How could Naunet have betrayed her own people like that? And him, too.

Zet's shoulders sagged. Never had he been so completely fooled. It was like he'd been blind, because he'd wanted to believe her. He realized then that he'd liked her. This was the worst blow of all.

The donkeys were walking side-by-side.

Zet glanced at Kissa, remembering she was half-Hyksos and didn't even know it. What would she say when she learned the truth? Would she feel betrayed by her mother?

Had that been part of Darius's plan? Had he seen Kissa's mother with Naunet, and decided she'd make the perfect decoy? Or had it been a fluke?

When they finally reached the canal, the sky was turning a pale shade of gray. Dawn would be here soon. The four paused at the reedy bank, and stared at one another in the growing light. They were a long way down from their earlier crossing.

"Better get this over with," Hui said, trying to urge Gray Ears forward.

"Wait," Zet said.

Hui glanced at him.

"I don't know if they can swim with two of us riding."

"I take it you have a plan?"

Zet nodded. "The girls ride. We swim alongside."

Hui looked at the river, as if seeing it with fresh eyes. Zet did the same. It churned and swirled, gurgling and spitting as it passed rocks and reeds on its way downstream. And who knew what lay under the burbling surface? Poisonous snakes. Crocodiles. Hippos.

"Come on," Zet said, not wanting to spend another moment thinking about it.

"I can't swim," Kissa blurted. "What if we fall off? The Princess can't either—"

"Look!" Princess Meritamon said. "Down there!"

The three kidnappers had just emerged onto the bank. They were tiny from this distance. Still, they turned and their shouts of triumph could be heard.

"Can you manage?" she asked Zet.

"Yes." Zet wound Brownie's bridle rope around his waist and tied it into a knot. Hui followed suit. Zet plunged in, pulling Brownie and the animal's precious cargo forward. Gray Ears clearly didn't want to be left behind. He responded to Hui's urging and got into the water.

The bank dropped off quickly. The current grabbed hold of Zet.

Only the bridle rope kept him from being carried away.

The swim was long and hard. Even the donkeys were being carried sideways. The current was much stronger here. No wonder Darius and Manu had chosen the other spot to cross. Zet could see them, along with the third man, on their donkeys swimming their way to the far bank.

But then the current ripped Zet and the others even faster. He went under.

The Princess pulled him, spluttering, to the surface. Moments later, the wild flow threw them against the bank. Zet stumbled for his footing, and then he was standing on land. Hui was right beside him. Up river, the men were still crossing.

"Which way is the harbor?" Princess Meritamon asked.

He pointed right.

"We have to cross their path?" she gasped. "They'll cut us off!"

"We'll try to skirt around them. They're still swimming, we'll make it."

29

A LAST STAND

Zet led Brownie by the rope into the towering rushes. Soon, the canal was lost from view. He stroked the donkey's matted fur. The animal was clearly exhausted.

"Just a little further." Feeling horrible, he climbed onto its back.

The Princess wrapped her arms around Zet's waist. It was clear escape was taking its toll. He could tell by her ragged breath she was in extreme pain.

"How much further?" she gasped.

"Not far," Zet lied.

When they burst out of the towering rushes, Zet's hopes fell. They were much further from the harbor than he ever expected. The pyramid rose, toy-sized, in the distance. They still had to pass by the construction site on the way.

The three men were sure to cut them off.

He prayed that medjay would appear out of the shadows, brandishing swords. Then he remembered what Darius had said, about the Hyksos trap.

As if to confirm his worst fears, none appeared.

A crazy idea came to him. A way to buy time. Maybe they'd have a chance.

"Head for the hill!" Zet told Hui.

"The pyramid," Hui said, clearly understanding Zet's plan.

Zet spoke into Brownie's ear, urging it forward. The animal was winded, snorting and shaking its furry head. But then, Brownie began to trot. Zet glanced back at Gray Ears. Reluctantly, the donkey started into a trot as well.

They rode for the giant structure. A cliff rose directly in front, forcing them left along the road. They reached the hairpin turn at the rear of the monument and the valley was momentarily lost from view. By the time they reached the front door and could see the kidnappers once again, the men were much closer.

Zet leaped to the ground and ran to open the giant door.

"Don't bother," Hui said. It's locked."

"Locked? You put your lock on this?"

Hui shrugged. "A priest of Osiris tells you to do something, you do it."

"Right. Fine. But can you open it?"

"What do I look like, an idiot?" Hui had dismounted and was moving his hands across the pyramid wall, counting the stones. He counted twelve to the right, and then three up. Then he dug his fingers into an all but invisible hole and pulled out a long, thin wooden rod. "Here it is. The key." He held it up.

"Just open it!" Princess Meritamon gasped.

"She's right, hurry."

On the broad plane below, the kidnappers were moments away. Zet could see their evil faces clearly in the moonlight.

Hui opened the door.

"Everyone inside," Zet said.

"But whose going for help?" Princess Meritamon cried.

"No one," Zet replied. "Close the door."

"I don't understand!" she gasped. "What are you doing?"

Hui said, "Yes, what are we doing?"

"Trust me. Just wait."

The four of them stood in the pitch-black entrance. Fear shuddered up Zet's spine. And not just because of Darius and Manu. They were in a sacred pyramid. Who knew what the gods would do?

He had to time it just right. The men must have reached the switch-back by now.

"Get ready," Zet whispered. "Princess Merit and Kissa, on my command, run out the door, in the opposite direction of the road. We'll all hide on the far side. Can you do it?"

"Yes," Princess Meritamon whispered in the dark.

"Now!" Zet whispered. He slid open the door softly. All four snuck out. The donkeys huddled a few yards away. Otherwise, the area was deserted. The four made it around the corner just as the three men approached from the far trail.

"I'm not going in there," Manu growled.

The second man agreed.

"You'll do what I tell you," Darius said.

A short argument ensued. Darius won.

Zet held his breath, listening as the door creaked open. He and the others had their backs pressed to the wall. Zet was breathing hard. He'd wait long enough for the men to get several yards inside. Then, he'd lock them in.

"Now!" he whispered to Hui.

They ran for the big door.

At that instant, one of the kidnappers emerged. Darius.

Zet's only weapon was surprise. He threw himself at Darius, who rocked unsteadily on his feet.

"Lock it!" Zet shouted.

Hui dodged a punch from Darius. From inside the pyramid, the other two men shouted. Their voices echoed up the dark passage and out through the gap. Zet tried to reach the open door, but Darius swung a meaty fist at his head. Zet ducked. Not fast enough. It clipped him and sent him sprawling.

Hui slammed the door and jammed the stick into the lock. Darius lunged at him as Hui pulled the stick out. Just before Darius got hold of him, Hui rolled sideways.

"Give me that stick!" shouted Darius.

Hui threw it to Zet. He caught it and rolled, sending Brownie and Gray Ears skittering backwards. Darius pounced on Hui and fastened him in a headlock. Zet's best friend cried out in pain.

Meanwhile, from inside, huge fists pounded the thick wood door.

Darius wrenched Hui around to face Zet and shouted, "Give me that stick or your friend's dead!"

"Pharaoh's soldiers are coming," Zet gasped, trying to call his bluff.

Darius laughed. "Nice try. Now give it to me!"

Hui was choking, his face crimson. Still, he gasped, "Run!"

"Run and I'll snap his neck," Darius snarled.

"No!" Zet cried, bargaining for time. "Wait, I'll do what you want."

"Open the door. NOW!"

"All right," Zet said. "Let him go and I'll open it."

"DO IT!" Darius barked. "You have until the count of three. One . . . two . . ."

Running forward, Zet made for the door. But before he got there, he tucked into a shoulder roll, flying head over heels. As he rolled over, he shot out his foot in a jarring kick. Darius had been ready, and jumped sideways.

The kick landed, but the force wasn't enough to knock him down.

Still, it was enough to make him loosen his grip on Hui.

Hui bit down on Darius's forearm. The big man yowled like an animal. He tried to shake Hui loose, but Hui wouldn't let go. Zet grabbed a stone and pelted it at Darius's head. The stone bounced off, but a trickle of blood started behind the man's ear. Darius ripped his forearm away from Hui and landed a punch on Hui's jaw.

The force sent Hui flying.

Zet sent a second stone winging toward Darius's head. Darius turned, and the rock hit him full in the face. Blood rushed from Darius's nose. Meanwhile, inside the pyramid, the two men kept pounding at the door, trying to break free. Darius staggered a moment. He regained his balance, and his dark eyes looked deadly.

"I'll kill you," he growled.

The third stone in Zet's hand never made it into the air. Darius was on him. The man knocked him down, and together they fell. Zet kicked and punched, but Darius was too big. The man's huge fist laid into Zet's stomach, knocking the wind out of him. A second blow slammed into Zet's jaw. Darius pulled his fist back a third time, but then his expression changed.

A shocked look came over his sunburnt face.

His eyes rolled up into his head.

He slumped onto Zet, as heavy as a bag of wet sand.

30

TRIUMPHANT DAWN

Zet tried to struggle out from under Darius. He wiggled sideways, far enough to see Hui standing over the limp kidnapper with a big rock in both hands.

"Should I hit him again?" Hui said.

"Uh, no, I think once was enough."

"And he thought he could beat us."

"Well, he's still beating me, I can't move," Zet said with a groan.

"Oh, right, hold on." Hui was smiling, even though he had a fat lip and his left eye was swollen almost shut.

Together, they got Darius onto his back. Then, deciding the man might choke from his nosebleed, they rolled him onto his side. Hui ran for some rope from the donkeys while Zet stood over Darius with the rock, just in case the thug came to.

Moments later, the kidnapper was trussed up like a duck ready for the cook pot.

The other two men still slammed against the pyramid door. They shouted now in more than just anger. They sounded terrified.

"Can they break that door down, do you think?" Zet said.

"No way. Not a chance. That door's as thick as a man's arm. They're not going anywhere."

"It's safe!" Zet called.

Princess Meritamon and Kissa peeked around the corner. A smile brightened Princess Merit's face. On the ground, Darius moaned. His eyes fluttered open. He tried to struggle upright, and then realized he was completely bound. Zet thought the Princess might shrink back, fearful of meeting her kidnapper face-to-face.

Even if he was all trussed up.

Instead, she cheered. A wonderful, loud cheer that echoed across the plains. Kissa joined in with a laugh that lit up her face. Watching the two of them celebrate was the best reward he could ever wish for.

Then to everyone's surprise, the donkeys brayed as if in agreement and they all started to laugh.

Finally, Hui sobered.

"We're not in the clear yet. At least, I'm not. I'm an escaped criminal."

"I don't think there will be a problem," Zet said. "Obviously Naunet hid the jewels in the river herself."

"Jewels?" Princess Merit asked.

"It's complicated."

"Well, on my honor as a Princess, I swear no harm will come to you. You saved me. You and Zet are heroes."

This cheered Hui up considerably.

"Come on, let's head back," Zet said.

"Good idea," Kissa said. "The Princess needs rest and water."

"You worry too much," she said with a laugh.

Zet said, "Actually, speaking of worrying, we need to approach the harbor carefully. We still don't know what happened to the medjay." His chest clenched, thinking of Merimose, the big Commander. What would they find?

He started toward Brownie, who flicked his tail and trotted over. He hoped the animals were up for another ride. It had been a long night.

"Looks like you've made a friend," Princess Merit said.

Zet stroked Brownie's nose. "We'd be dead without these guys."

The Princess let him help her up onto Brownie's back. She was so easy to be around that he'd nearly forgotten who she was. But then a wave of awe swept over him and he shook his head in amazement.

The sturdy donkey set out, with Zet walking alongside. The group wound back down toward the harbor, sticking to the shadows. They stayed off the road, and took the long way around.

Princess Merit insisted on hearing the whole story, so Zet and Hui talked in low voices, telling her and Kissa everything, from the Queen Mother's visit, to the boat ride, to Hui's discovery of the jewels, and breaking him out of prison.

The girls listened in amazement, laughing quietly and asking questions. The only thing Zet kept to himself was Kissa's story, and the truth about her birth. It wasn't his to tell.

Zet and Hui left the girls hidden near some date trees and covered the last distance alone. If Hyksos soldiers had attacked, who knew what they'd find.

Pharaoh's boat stood at anchor, white sails fluttering in the gentle breeze. In front of the boat, clustered along the harbor, stood a band of strange looking men. They wore foreign clothes, and their broad shoulders and arms were bloodied and bruised. Hui grabbed Zet's arm, his fingers like pincers. A bolt of horror shot down Zet's spine.

Hyksos warriors.

Then his eyes went to their sword belts.

They were empty.

He frowned. Suddenly, he noticed how close together the men stood. Realization dawned. This wasn't an attack. They hadn't taken control of Pharaoh's boat. The men were tied together by ropes.

They were prisoners.

The dark head of Merimose became visible on the far side of the group. Zet's heart leaped. The captain was alive. Still, his arm was bandaged from wrist to shoulder. He looked haggard with worry.

"We're safe!" Zet gasped, sending a prayer of thanks to the gods.

He and Hui ran back for the girls. When they returned, Merimose spun at the donkeys' approach. When he saw the four of them, he looked like he almost sagged with relief. Then his eyes lit up with joy.

But before either Zet or Merimose could speak, there came a loud roar of delight.

The Mighty Bull appeared from between a pack of medjay. He shouted with undisguised relief at the sight of his favorite daughter. Striding forward, he lifted her from Brownie's back and held her in his big arms as if she were a child of five, and not a grown girl.

"All right, I'm safe! Let go!" she scolded, but she was laughing.

WHILE PHARAOH REJOICED, Zet learned from Merimose that the medjay had tracked the band of Hyksos. They'd been lying in wait for the handover. If things went wrong, they planned to kill Pharaoh, and Princess Meritamon as well. There had been a long, drawn out skirmish, and the medjay won by the skin of their teeth.

"You were wise to approach with caution. Things could have turned out much differently," Merimose said.

Zet let this sink in. They might still be running. "Then I guess we make a good team," he said.

At this, Merimose looked chagrined, but laughed.

Zet told Merimose about Darius and the others, still back at the pyramid. Men were dispatched to round them up.

"And take the priest," Merimose told the men. "Being Pharaoh's holy burial place, I'm sure he'll want to be involved in purging it from the likes of those three."

"There's someone else," Zet said.

Merimose gave him a quizzical look. "This is quite the morning."

Zet felt a pang of sadness as he described the shed where they'd left Naunet. Beside him Hui was fidgeting nervously, despite the Princess's earlier assurances.

Zet said, "She was the one who stole the jewels."

"She deserves what she gets," Hui said. "Trying to frame me for her theft!"

"We'll find her," Merimose said.

"Thank you," Zet said.

Merimose patted him with his good arm. "You did well." And then he was gone.

Morning light spread warm fingers through the camp, filling it with golden light. Everyone had come out to see Pharaoh. It wasn't often one got to stand in the presence of a living god. The camp stood at a respectful distance, watching in breathless silence.

People were talking about Princess Meritamon, too.

"Can you believe it was her all along? She visited our mess tent three times before she was kidnapped. I stood behind her in line!"

"I knew it was the Princess!" someone whispered.

"You did not, you dolt," whispered another.

Glancing around, Zet wondered where the architect was. Then he spotted Senna in conversation with a formally dressed man. Pharaoh's personal scribe, no doubt. Did Senna ever stop working?

"Come on," Zet said to Hui.

They headed over.

"Ah, my runners," Senna said. "Now, I have plenty of messages to go out today. Seeing that the Princess is found, it's time you got to work."

Hui opened his mouth. Nothing came out.

"Er—" Zet began, "We'd love to, but we have to get going. Home and all that."

"Home!" Senna cried, his feathery brows waving in the breeze. "Ridiculous! Do you have any idea how much—"

Zet said, "I think I hear Commander Merimose calling us!"

He grabbed Hui's arm and took off.

"I was joking, boys!" Senna shouted.

Zet glanced back. Senna, the old trickster, wore a toothy grin.

31

HOMEWARD

The morning celebration continued into breakfast. Entering the mess tent and seeing the camp's happy faces, Zet realized he'd had no idea how unhappy and concerned people had been about the kidnapping. It would have been worse if they'd known then the Priestess was the Princess.

They were a transformed group. It was as if a hidden weight had been lifted.

"I knew you were pulling one over on me!" shouted Jafar, laughing and grabbing Zet around his shoulders and scuffing up Zet's hair. "Not a friend of the medjay, huh?"

Hui grinned—fat-lip and all—and was bursting with pride. With his swollen eye, he looked like a scruffy, heroic dog.

"And you, too!" Jafar shouted. "Kemet's best young jeweler, the architect's *runner*? Ha!"

They finally stumbled outside, grinning, their backs sore from so many construction workers pounding them with congratulations.

"This has been crazy. Fun, scary, exciting," Zet said. "But you know what? I'm suddenly really looking forward to getting home."

"Me, too," Hui said. "Speaking of that, how exactly *do* we get home?"

"Good question. But before we find out, we need to visit Brownie and Gray Ears." He pulled a handful of honeyed apricots from his pocket and grinned.

Later, they were wandering along the wharf toward their crooked tent, when the flap was thrust aside. A man in a gold embroidered tunic had Zet and Hui's packs in his arms.

"You will follow me," the man said. "We embark shortly."

"I guess that's our ride," Zet said, glancing at Hui.

But when the man in the gold embroidered tunic led them to Pharaoh's gangplank, bowed and motioned them on board, Zet and Hui shot each other looks of disbelief.

"Is this really happening?" Hui whispered.

"We're sailing into Thebes on the royal barge?" Zet whispered back.

Hui whooped, they performed their secret handshake, and Zet was about to do some completely ridiculous happy dance when he noticed Princess Meritamon on deck.

"Tell me you'll teach me how to do that!" she said, laughing.

Zet was suddenly reminded of the day he'd seen her at the Opet festival, surrounded by people vying for her attention. He thought of her grandmother, too, and felt a rush of happiness. The Princess would be home for her party, and the world would be whole.

"All right," Zet said, laughing.

"I'll show it to my handmaidens. They're always far too serious."

"Maybe I could teach them a few magic tricks," Hui added. "That would definitely lighten them up."

The three of them glanced at the Princess's boat, which was getting ready to set sail and follow them south. A woman stood on deck with her arm around Kissa. It was Kissa's mother, the woman from the cell.

She spotted Zet and a grateful smile lit her eyes.

Had she told Kissa, yet? They'd have a lot to talk about.

"Kissa's my dearest friend. I don't want her mother to tell her," Princess Meritamon said suddenly. "As far as I'm concerned, she's Egyptian. But I suppose she deserves the truth."

. . .

LUNCH AND DINNER on board were royal affairs. They ate on plates trimmed with gold and drank from cups made of real glass. Every food imaginable appeared, and all of it delicious. Zet was eating too fast to taste it!

"So," Pharaoh said. "You hid in my pyramid?" Living god that he was, he laughed like any human. "I'll be thinking of that when I go off into eternity!"

"Did you know donkeys can swim?" Princess Merit asked.

"Brownie and Gray Ears deserve medals," Zet said.

Princess Meritamon and Hui agreed.

"I think that's a grand idea," Pharaoh said. "Medals, and we'll make sure they get the best life a donkey could ever wish for!"

Later, the Great Bull pulled Zet and Hui aside. "You saved my daughter. For that, I and the gods are eternally grateful."

Zet knew those words of praise would stay with him for the rest of his life.

THAT EVENING, he stood by the rail and watched the water trail behind them. He was thinking of Naunet. *Why had she done it?*

The princess appeared, walking slowly. Her limp was barely visible. She leaned on her elbows beside him.

"All this time," she said, "I've been racking my brain, wondering if I'd treated Naunet poorly."

Zet rubbed his thumb against the polished rail, staring down at it. "I don't believe that for a minute."

She was silent.

"I just wish I knew why she did it," he said.

Stars sparkled in the dark water.

"We were friends," she said. "I thought we were. But I knew there was a lot of tension between her and the others. Naunet had a way of treating everything like a competition. One thing I must tell you—she was the one who insisted Kissa be there on the day we were kidnapped. And she insisted Kissa bring her healing herbs. So I suppose she did care a little."

Zet sighed. "I was thinking about Darius. Maybe he threatened her?"

"That's possible," the Princess said. "I'll be sure it's raised when she faces trial."

It was the only bitter drop in the wonderful outcome. The Princess was safe. They'd averted a new war. Zet was determined to be happy.

ONCE THEY REACHED THEBES, the sight of his familiar city lightened his spirits.

No one knew of the kidnapping plot, but as Pharaoh's boat neared shore, people spotted the white and gold sails. They began to gather, running along the watersteps, appearing out of nearby streets and buildings. Soon, a crowd of cheering citizens stood to welcome their Pharaoh and his daughter.

"I can't forget to give you this," Zet said, pulling the golden cord with the Queen Mother's ring over his neck and handing it to Princess Meritamon.

She cradled it in her hands, her eyes shining. "She was right about you. I am forever in your debt for saving my life."

Zet didn't know how to answer. Instead, he just bowed low.

After bidding goodbye to Pharaoh, Zet and Hui ran down the gangplank. They sprinted through the familiar streets, glad to be back. When they reached their own block, the street was quiet.

It was as if nothing had happened.

Except a lot had. And now, to Zet, the city seemed smaller. Still wonderful, but different. It was amazing how a few days could change you. He grinned when he spotted his front door, and saw movement through the open window.

"We're home!" Zet shouted.

The front door flew open.

Everyone was hugging and laughing.

Hui and Kat had a tearful reunion—on Kat's part—Hui was too busy showing off his bruised face to be tearful.

Zet's mother ran to fetch Hui's family from their house a block away. Everyone piled into Zet's house. Their story was told over a huge brunch.

The only part Zet left out was the part about Naunet. He'd never told Hui about her, and he never would.

When a knock sounded on the door, Zet ran to answer.

A royal courier stood there, a boy around Zet's age. The courier eyed Zet strangely, obviously surprised to be delivering news to a place like this.

Kat appeared. "What is it?"

"A message," the courier said, holding out a leather bound scroll. He looked doubtful. "Should I read it for you?"

"No. Thank you." Kat took it. "I can read it on my own."

The courier's brows shot up. Then he left.

"What does it say?" Zet said.

"Hold on! Let me open it," Kat replied.

Hui squeezed between them. "Who's it from?"

Kat scanned the contents, and her eyes widened. "The palace! We're invited to the palace, next week. To see the Queen Mother!"

"Us?" Zet said. "That's crazy!"

"She wants to thank you in person. Wait, and there's a note from the Princess—she hopes we'll sit with her in her royal box at her birthday celebration." Now, it was Kat's turn to freak out. "What will I wear?" she practically screamed.

Zet covered his ears and rolled his eyes.

Hui grinned. "I told you I saw a future in this! Didn't I? Secret Agent Zet and his trusty partner Hui win again!"

"By the way," Zet's mother interjected, "Old Teni came by, said something about her roof?"

"Uh oh," Zet said, glancing at his best friend. But then he started to laugh.

Already the sights and smells and dangers of Abydos were fading. They were home. With their families, the people they cared about most. Everything was back to normal.

They really had won.

HISTORICAL NOTE FROM THE AUTHOR

Although this is a story, Zet, Kat, and their friends' world is much as it would have been. Egyptians kept good notes. They loved to write things down. Using ancient records, we can imagine what life was like back then—from what they wore to the houses they lived in, from their boats to the way they built big structures.

I want to mention the writing style I used. It's common to imagine people spoke more formally in ancient times, but we have no evidence of this. In fact, ancient Egyptians loved parties and games, they faced social struggles, and were even guilty of graffiti. Keeping in mind that neither formal nor casual English would be correct as English didn't exist, I veered away from the formal to make the story more accessible.

Abydos is one of the most important archaeological sites in Egypt. King Narmer (also thought to be Menes), Egypt's first pharaoh, was buried there. The pyramid of Ahmose I was the only pyramid built at Abydos. Although it has mostly crumbled away, its remains can still be visited today.

Scott Peters has always had a fascination for all things ancient Egyptian. Scott has created over 300 museum, science center and theme park installations for such places as the Smithsonian, the Washington Children's Museum, Walt Disney World and Paramount Pictures.

Scott hosts a blog for kids, teachers, and fans of ancient Egypt here:

www.egyptabout.com

Come visit!

The Complete Zet Mystery Series

Mystery of the Egyptian Scroll

Mystery of the Egyptian Amulet

Mystery of the Egyptian Temple

Mystery of the Egyptian Mummy

More Great Ancient Egypt Reads

Secret of the Egyptian Curse

Mummies: 101 Ancient Egypt Mummy Facts

The I Escaped Series

I Escaped North Korea!

I Escaped The California Camp Fire

I Escaped the World's Deadliest Shark Attack